WOMEN OF THE KALEVALA

Women of the Kalevala

Stories Based on the Great Finnish Epic

Mary Caraker

North Star Press of St. Cloud, Inc.

Dedication

To
Miles and Emily
of the coming generation.

Acknowledgements

The excerpts from the *Kalevala* are taken from Eino Friberg's translation, published by Otava Publishing Company, Ltd., Helsinki, Finland, in cooperation with the Finnish North American Literature Society, Inc., Turku, Finland, 1988. Used with permission.

Library of Congress Cataloging-in-Publication Data

Caraker, Mary.
    Women of the Kalevala / Mary Caraker.
    128 p. 23 cm.
    Eight tales based on characters appearing in the Finnish epic, the
Kalevala.
    ISBN 0-87839-106-1 (pbk.)
    1. Epic poetry, Finnish—Adaptations. 2. Women—Finland—
Mythology—Fiction. 3. Fantastic fiction, American. I. Kalevala.
II. Title.
PS3553.A638W66 1996
811'.54--dc20   96-26021
                                                       CIP

Printed in the United States of America by Versa Press, Inc., East Peoria, Illinois.

Published by: North Star Press of St. Cloud, Inc.
                     P.O. Box 451
                     St. Cloud, Minnesota

Contents

ഗ ✤ ര

Preface

෨ ✿ ෬

For readers unfamiliar with the Finnish folk epic, the *Kalevala*, a brief introduction will set the context for these eight tales. For those with further interest, I recommend my principal source, the Friberg translation of the poem.

Elias Lönnrot in 1835 published the collection of runes, or Finnish folk songs, that became the *Kalevala*. This long, digressive poem relates the adventures of three mythical heroes, Väinämöinen, Lemminkäinen and Ilmarinen, as they live, love and wage war in a misty, unspecified, pagan medieval time. Its background is the feud between the heroes' people of Kaleva and the inhabitants of Pohjola, an unknown and frightening country to the north. It follows the heroes as they search for brides, recounts the quest for the Sampo, a magical talisman of prosperity, and ends with the introduction of Christianity.

Much has been written about the *Kalevala* as a mirror of the life of the early Finns, and about its significance to Finnish pride and nationalism. The heroes have been celebrated in art and music as well as in literature, their voices clearly heard and interpreted through the years.

More muted are the voices of the women characters, even though they hold important roles in the *Kalevala* action. When we read of stolen brides and of lonely lives on isolated farms, it seems to me that those voices are clamoring to be heard. The wives and sisters and daughters have their own stories, in most cases more poignant than those of the men, and deserving to be told from their own viewpoints.

Though it abounds in supernatural elements, the *Kalevala* also presents men and women as they live ordinary, everyday lives. The women, especially, can be recognized as real people, with hopes and joys and sorrows which we can understand today. In telling their stories, I have attempted to place Aino and Kylli and the others in an even more realistic context than that of the poem. I beg the pardon of *Kalevala* purists for altering certain events and adding others in order to do this, but I was looking through the eyes of my characters, and their voices directed me.

One

Aino

ဆ ❀ ෬

"Why do you weep, my little Aino,
Since you have so great a suitor,
Going to a great estate . . ."

The Kalevala, Runo 3

AINO CONTINUED TO CRY, crouched on the outer stairway that led to her family's living quarters above the barn, and nothing her mother said could comfort her. "Such a distinguished person," her mother repeated, and when Aino did not respond, the older woman's tone grew sharper. "You should be proud to bring such honor to our family."

Aino buried her wet face in her apron. Of course she knew the fame of Väinämöinen, the great spellsinger from Kaleva. She had heard of his riches—his boats and sleds and stables of horses, his vast fields and the full coffers in his storerooms. But she also knew that he was old and wrinkled and gray-bearded. The other maidens of her Lapp village giggled about him; how, for all his reputation, he had never been able to win himself a wife.

Anger replaced her tears as Aino thought of her betraying brother. How could he have done it? Bartering her as if she were a horse or a cow or even a pig! Hot words rose to her lips, but she swallowed them when she uncovered her face and saw him still leaning, flushed with shame, against his broken sleigh. Joukahainen had come driving home from the south like a madman, crashing purposely, it seemed, into the barn. Since delivering his news, he had not dared to meet his sister's eyes, and now he continued to stare fixedly at the toes of his boots. "I had no choice," he mumbled. "I only did it to save my life."

"Would you rather your brother had smothered in quicksand?" their mother said. She folded her arms across her ample bosom. "Enough of this. What's done is done, and I say it's not a bad thing. Now go wash your face like a good girl, and put on a better dress." She looked anxiously across the barnyard and fields to the spot where, barely visible from the house, a trail entered the green expanse of forest. "He should be here before dark."

1

Before dark. Yes, the old man would be eager to inspect his prize, Aino thought bitterly as she trudged up the wooden stairs. Inside the dark, log-walled room with its rough plank floor she crossed to her curtained alcove and collapsed, again in misery, on the straw pallet she shared at night with her younger sister.

She cried until she had no more tears, until she was drained of feeling, as helpless and inert as a sack of spilled grain.

Her first anguish spent, Aino allowed her anger toward her brother to diminish, too. Perhaps it hadn't all been Joukahainen's fault. At least not the outcome. Väinämöinen had no need to punish him so severely. Joukahainen was only a rash lad, praised too much by their neighbors for his singing skills and eager to test them against the greatest spellsinger of all. He had been determined to journey south and challenge Väinämöinen, and nothing his mother or father had said could dissuade him.

Of course it had been no contest. Väinämöinen had sung his foolish rival into a swamp, and had refused to reverse the spell until Joukahainen had promised him what he desired most. Aino found a fresh source of tears at the thought of the lecherous old man. He had a beard down to his waist, she had heard. The body of a fat sea cow and a face like a troll. What good would be a fine house and a soft bed with linen sheets, married to such a one!

Light footsteps approached, and Aino's sister Lilja knelt beside her. Lilja was only ten, a dark, gangly child, with as yet no promise of her older sister's beauty. Aino, at seventeen, was the flower of the southern Lapp countryside, with skin as fair as that of any Kalevalander, eyes as blue as the floating ice of the winter ocean, and braids that were longer and thicker than those of any maiden in their border province.

Now, however, Aino's eyes were red-rimmed and her famed complexion blotched from crying. Lilja reached out a hand to stroke one of the disordered braids, and Aino sat up abruptly and embraced her. "He'll take me away," she said with a hiccup. "Far away from you and Mother and Father." The hiccuping became a wail of despair. "How can I go to a strange country like Kaleva? How can I leave everything I've ever known?" She hugged Lilja tighter and moaned into her thin shoulder. "Just think: I'll never again get to pick strawberries on the hill behind the cornfield, or dance around the *Juhannus* fire. Someone else will feed my calf in the mornings and ride my horse through the woods. And you—you'll grow up without me, and before long you'll forget me!"

"I won't," Lilja declared fiercely. "I'll never forget you. And Mama says that Väinämöinen—"

At Aino's sudden stiffening, Lilja stopped her tongue.

"Don't even say that name," Aino warned.

2

Lilja broke the awkward silence. "Anyway, you'll come back to visit, won't you?"

"At her husband's pleasure," their mother said, parting the curtain and scowling down at Aino. "I told you to get yourself dressed. We have too much to do, with such an important visitor arriving any minute, for you to lie around sulking. Lilja, run along to the milkhouse and fetch me some cream, and then you can help me with the cakes. Aino, when you're ready, you can go to the birch grove and cut new switches for the sauna." Her stern expression softened slightly. "And don't waste tears over strawberries. They grow bigger in Kaleva, I've heard, than they do here. And as the mistress of Väinämöinen's house, you won't even have to pick them yourself. There'll be pitchers of cream—more than you can ever use, and tubs of fresh, sweet butter. You'll eat white bread like the foreigners, cut in thin slices, and as for the *Juhannus* fire, you'll be a married woman and through with all that kind of larking about."

Aino set her lips in a thin line and made no reply. Her mother laid out the blue dress Aino had been saving for *Juhannus*, a belt with copper tassels from her own clothes chest, a set of red ribbons and a beaded necklace. "We don't want Väinämöinen to think he's made a bad bargain, do we? Now put these on, and if you should meet him on the trail, a little smile might even win your father a new cow or two."

Aino dutifully adorned herself, but her heart was as heavy in her breast as her father's huge grindstone. From the doorway she cast a sorrowful glance backwards at the familiar room: the benches and table she had scrubbed so often, set already with polished tankards, her father's and brother's crossbows on the wall pegs, and between the door and window the red wall hanging on which she had worked so many winters. Simple and homely and smelling more than slightly of the barn—not to be compared with the fabled splendor of Väinämöinen's southern manor. If only . . . if only her bridegroom were someone else. Aino had always known that some day she would have to leave her father's house, but she had imagined it so differently. If only the man she was going now to meet were someone her own age, with red hair and a shy smile. Someone like the young fisherman she had danced with last Midsummer Eve, whom she had dreamed of for a whole year while sewing the blue dress.

His eyes, she recalled, had gleamed as brightly as the embers scattered by the bonfire. His smile had been as warm, and his hand, when it clasped hers and swung her in the twirling steps, had felt as strong and secure as her father's own. His name was Toivo, he had told her during a lull in the dancing, for he had not left her side until her mother had advanced upon them with swishing skirts and angry eyes and pulled Aino away.

"Don't waste your time with that one," the woman had scolded. "I've been asking around about him. His father has a broken-down fishing boat and a load of debts. The mother"—she pointed to a raddled-looking woman far gone in drink—"as you can see, it's not a family you'd care to join."

It's not his fault, Aino had wanted to protest, but at her mother's I'll-brook-no-nonsense expression she had held her peace.

In the next dance, when they had come together briefly again, Toivo had whispered something—a question, it had seemed—before they were swept apart. Aino wasn't sure what he had said, and she hadn't answered. Her mother had made the family leave early, and Aino still didn't know what the question had been. Since then she had relived the evening over and over, and she was almost sure he had said, "Could you ever like me?"

Or maybe—and the possibility made her face flame—maybe the word had been, "love."

Now, she would never have the opportunity to answer. She would never dance in the blue dress around a bonfire. And Toivo. . . .

She would have to put thoughts of him away forever, Aino told herself. She knew in the rational part of her mind that her mother was right, that there would be nothing but hardship for her in a fisherman's hut, that she should feel lucky to have the prospect of an easeful future. And maybe . . . maybe all the girlish gossip about Väinämöinen wasn't true. If he was such a great magic-singer, couldn't he spell himself young and handsome, especially for his wedding?

But he had never done so before, and Aino expected that it was as foolish a hope as were her dreams of the red-haired fisherman. She closed the door and descended the stairs with dragging feet.

The barnyard was still muddy from the spring rains, and Aino lifted her skirt and slipped on clogs to cross it. At the calf pen her own little white-faced pet bleated and stuck a wet muzzle through the slats.

"No, I won't stop to play with you," Aino said. "There'll be no more of that, not ever, so you can just go ahead and cry."

The calf's plaintive bellowing followed her as she fastened the barn-yard gate behind her and circled the new-sprouted fields to enter the forest. There, in the thick shadows, the evergreens whispered to her, the pines of sad farewells and the firs of an unwilling journey. As she crushed the soft humus under her feet, she seemed to be treading on her own dreams.

Aino's eyes were wet again when she reached the birch hollow, but she scrubbed away her tears and set determinedly to work. The sleigh trail led directly through the copse, and for all her mother's hints she had no wish to meet Väinämöinen there alone. It would be difficult enough, in the shelter of her family.

Perhaps he would have an accident, she thought—there were always bears in the woods. She breathed easier for a moment before she realized that such a great spellsinger could surely protect himself. No, he would come, and soon. Aino glanced nervously in the direction of the trail and told herself again to hurry.

She had broken off several low growing, leafy branches suitable for sauna switches when she heard a crashing not far off. Before she had time to hide herself, a horse and sleigh came bursting into the grove.

"Whoa there," the driver shouted, and Aino watched, frozen, as he descended from the sleigh.

It was all true—all her worst imaginings. Väinämöinen was a man huge with the fleshy roundness of age, his face like a great seamed pumpkin surrounded by gray moss that covered his barrel chest. When he removed his cap in courtesy and bowed to her, his bald pate gleamed like an upturned butter tub, and his rheumy eyes, almost lost in crinkled folds of flesh, gleamed too as he studied her with an appreciation that sent fingers of cold up her spine.

"You must be little Aino, come to meet me," he croaked. He held out his arms. "And dressed so finely. Come, let me see how prettily you have bedecked yourself for me."

When Aino did not step forward willingly, the old man seized her with gnarled hands and turned her about slowly in front of him. "Ah, yes," he said with a whistling breath. "Beautiful, indeed—your brother did not mislead me." He released her arms and fingered the beaded necklace on her breast. "And all this for me. For me, alone." His fingers strayed, and Aino jerked backwards.

The old spellsinger chuckled. "A shy one, eh? Better and better. Because from now on you need not wear this pretty necklace for anyone but me." He reached for her braids and slid them through his hands until he came to the ribboned ends. "Or tie these ribbons for anyone else to see."

As he reached for her belt with the copper tassels, Aino leaped backwards, out of his grasp. It was insufferable! She couldn't bear another touch, and without thinking, she tore the tassels loose and threw them on the ground. Her necklace followed, and then the red silk ribbons. "There!" she shouted, trampling them underfoot. "I'll never wear those again for you, or for anyone else either!"

Väinämöinen stared open-mouthed as Aino continued to rage, her eyes brimming and her cheeks red flags of revolt. "I don't need any such trinkets, from you or anyone." She tore at her dress, ripping a sleeve. "Or fancy dresses, or your slivers of white bread. I'd rather go in rags and live on crusts, just to stay here with Mother and Father." Her voice broke on a sob, and she turned and ran, pushing herself heedlessly through the branches, away from the trail and not looking back.

She heard her suitor's horse and sleigh as he continued on to the farm, but she did not follow. She wandered at the edge of the forest, keeping out of sight, as she watched him welcomed and received into the house. She waited until she saw him come out again, accompanied by her father, the two of them apparently companionable as old friends as they crossed the yard and entered the smoking sauna.

So the match was still on. She had hoped that Väinämöinen might have been put off by the idea of an unwilling bride, especially one given to displays of temper, but her mother had undoubtedly smoothed it over. Aino felt helpless as a fish caught in a net. And as cold, too, as the afternoon shadows lengthened and the night wind blew from the sea. She held the edges of her sleeve together as she crossed the fields with slumped shoulders and heavy feet, this time treading heedlessly over the new shoots.

Joukahainen met her at the gate. "Where have you been?" He shook his head and frowned. "Mother's really upset—you'd better be careful."

Aino only shrugged. Her brother noticed the torn sleeve and his frown deepened. "What happened? Did he—"

"No, I tore it myself," Aino said crossly. "Though if I hadn't—would you care?"

"Of course I would," Joukahainen protested. "I wouldn't want you to come to harm. Surely you know that." He peered intently into her face. "This marriage—it'll be for the best, you'll see. You may not think so now, but in a year or two—wait and see. Väinämöinen's old, and he'll dote on you."

"I know," Aino said drily.

Joukahainen ignored the irony in her tone. "Then you don't hate me?"

Aino didn't answer, but she allowed him to swing her over the gate as he used to do when she was smaller, and she did not shake off his arm as he led her to the house.

"Väinämöinen has promised to teach me some of his magic spells," he chattered as if there had been no division between them. "Just think: maybe some day I'll be as famous as he is."

Joukahainen had always considered himself first, Aino thought. She knew she would get no help from him in escaping from the net.

And certainly not from her mother, who was only concerned with drawing the webstrings more tightly. "I hope your brother talked some sense into you," she said when Aino came inside. "Väinämöinen called you a skittish colt, but fortunately he wasn't angry. I assured him that you'd behave better, so don't make me have to apologize to him again."

Her mother had prepared a feast, Aino saw. The table was lavishly spread with loaves of bread and rounds of butter, a dish of pork and another of salmon, and an array of cream cakes. Lilja, in a clean white apron over her best dress, tried to sneak a cake and received a slap from her mother, who shooed both girls to the other end of the room. "I swear I've raised a couple of hoydens," she complained, raising her eyes to the ceiling. "May it please Ukko to help me get them both safely married before they grow any worse!"

Lilja and Aino hid behind their curtain. "Married!" Lilja whispered with horror. "Never!"

Aino grasped both of her sister's hands. "You've seen him, then?"

"Yes." Lilja's eyes were round as cart wheels. "He's so . . ."

"Ugly," she finished just as Aino mouthed, "old."

They continued to hold hands. "What will you do?" Lilja whispered.

Aino lowered herself to the pallet, where she sat hugging her knees. "What *can* I do?"

"Lilja, help your sister mend her dress," their mother shouted. "Then both of you come out here and sit quietly, like well-mannered girls."

Aino could barely hold the needle, and Lilja, too, sewed with clumsy fingers. The repaired sleeve was noticeably crooked and bore a stain from a pricked finger, but Aino covered both shoulders with a kerchief and her mother nodded approvingly. Soon a kerchief would cover her hair as well, Aino thought, watching her mother's cloth-covered head as she flitted about the room, straightening a dish here, a bench there. A wife's crowning beauty was to be seen only by her husband, and Aino felt a moment of nausea as she recalled Väinämöinen's knobby fingers caressing her braids.

Aino and Lilja sat stiffly at the table's far end. "Now remember, you are to show him proper respect," their mother said as she placed a cushion upon the honored seat by the fireplace. "He wants the wedding as soon as possible." She smiled at Aino, but it was a smile that made Aino shrink back upon the bench. Joukahainen came in with a pitcher of beer and filled the tankards, and a few minutes later the father of the family and Väinämöinen came in together.

Both men were still red from the sauna and refused the bench by the fire. They sat together under the window, and in the late, slanting rays of sunlight, the comparison between Aino's vigorous, black-bearded father and her aged bridegroom was a cruel one.

At her mother's signal, Aino served the men beer and then filled a plate for her suitor. He rewarded her with an approving leer, and then, to her great relief, returned to conversation with her father.

The meal seemed interminable to Aino, especially whenever she felt Väinämöinen's eyes upon her. She pushed her food around on her plate, unable to swallow a morsel. Lilja cast her frequent glances of pity, and Joukahainen wouldn't look at her at all. If only she could slide under the table, as she had done as a child! If only she could disappear.

Finally the last cake was eaten, but Aino's ordeal was not yet over. Her mother and father begged Väinämöinen for music, and he was glad to comply. He had brought his lap harp, and Joukahainen fetched it from the sled. Aino settled back with the others to listen, not expecting to be entertained—how could she, by such a bridegroom?—but warned by her mother's sharp glance she folded her hands and assumed an expression of proper courtesy.

Väinämöinen placed the harp on his knees, tightened its five strings and plucked a few clear notes. When he began to play, Aino straightened in her seat as her expression altered to one of unfeigned amazement.

She had never heard such music from that or any other instrument. It was pure magic: sunlight on rippling water, birds in blossoming trees, the flames of a hearth, children's laughter and her own captured dreams.

When he began to sing, in a voice equally magical, Aino closed her eyes and allowed herself to be carried away. He sang of Kaleva, with its lakes and forests and mighty rivers, and she could see clearly everything he described. He sang of Väinölä, his own province, where the fish jumped into nets and the game into snares, where crops sprouted almost as you sowed in the long summer days and where even the winter snows fell softly and sweetly. She shuddered when he sang of Pohjola, the great, dark, evil land, and cheered when he sang of how he had defeated raids by the Pohjolanders with his powerful charms. When he sang, she forgot about his age and appearance and saw him only as a valiant hero.

He stopped for a drink, and when he had refreshed himself Aino joined the others in begging him to continue. This time he sang of the ocean, of wondrous vessels he had built and storm tossed waves he had quelled, and Aino's eyes flew open.

She had seen Toivo, fighting the sea in a leaky fishing boat.

Väinämöinen's spell was broken. He was an old man again, trying to seduce her with his music. She clenched her fists, hating him, and refused to listen to the rest of his songs. Nothing now could blind her to his person, and when he finally put away his harp and began to discuss the wedding with her parents, the sickness rose up once more in her throat.

"Three days," Aino's mother said. "It will take that long to prepare the feast and get word to all the neighbors. And surely"—with a small bow to Väinämöinen—"you'll want guests of your own."

"No, forget all that," the old man said. "It's too far to send to Väinölä, and I don't need a gabble of curiosity seekers. All I want is right here"—he favored Aino with another of his leering smiles—"and I've waited for this happiness too long already. We can even dispense with the wedding feast—what you have here on this table is fine. Joukahainen can go to the village for witnesses, and we can have the wedding tomorrow."

"Why not?" Aino's father said, beaming. "Who needs all the fuss and expense?" He brought his fist down on the table. "Tomorrow it is!"

Why doesn't anyone ask me? Aino wanted to shout. She might as well be one of Lilja's wooden dolls, without feelings. *Papa, look at me,* she begged him silently. It's the same Aino, the same little chicken you used to ride on your shoulders, the same pretty snowbird you rescued from the nettles and from the muddy pond and promised to protect forever.

How could he have forgotten? How could he sit drinking with the horrible old man, fawning on him, all but licking his boots at the promise of a new horse and wagon? Aino had thought to appeal to him in private, but when Väinämöinen left to visit the privy and her father, flushed with ale, twirled her about and called her his treasure trove, his laughter drowned her protests.

Väinämöinen returned, and there were more toasts. When the drunken men finally retreated noisily to their beds, in her curtained corner Aino lay awake beside Lilja and tried to think of ways to escape. It would be easy enough to run away, but what then? There was no one who would provide her refuge, and in the woods she could not survive alone.

It was hopeless, she granted, as morning light crept through the curtain. Their mother roused Lilja, but Aino pretended sleep and was left alone. She closed her ears to the commotion—tables being moved, brooms slapping, a fire roaring. She tried to think of nothing, that the preparations were not for her, that she had left her body and nothing mattered any more.

It worked until her mother parted the curtain and told her it was time to get ready. Aino saw a room with walls and floor still wet from scrubbing, a white cloth on the table and a mat of fresh boughs before the door. A haunch of meat sizzled in the fireplace, and fresh loaves cooled on the window sill.

"It *will* be a proper wedding," Aino's mother said. "Your brother went early to the village, so guests should be arriving before long. Here"—she unhooked two keys from the bundle at her waist. "You can't get married in a ruined dress. Go to the big storehouse on the hill and open up the back room. You'll find a chest there—this key will open it—and inside, my own wedding clothes.

"Run along now," she insisted when Aino did not move. "And no more of that sniveling."

The tears ran unchecked down Aino's cheeks, but she obediently took the keys. Her mother smiled, wiped Aino's cheeks with her apron and pushed her towards the door. "You'll cheer up when you see what's in the chest. The Moonmaid herself gave it to me, when I was as innocent as you, and I only wore the precious things for the three days of my own wedding feast." The older woman's eyes misted, and for a moment she looked as young and beautiful as her daughter. "It was the happiest time of my life."

"But you were marrying a man you loved," Aino said, thinking of her still handsome, black-haired father as he must have looked then.

The familiar, tired face returned. "Yes, but I had no idea of the life I was going to. The farm wasn't cleared then, and the house was a sod hut. We had no one to help us, and I had to work with your father like a man, burning fields and plowing. In bad years—and there were plenty of those—I knew the taste of famine bread." She ran work-worn hands over her apron. "Ukko be praised you will be spared all that."

Further protests, Aino knew, would be useless. At the top of the stairs, a quick glance around the farmyard reassured her that Väinämöinen was nowhere in sight. She hurried down, across the yard, through the gate and up the storehouse hill.

It would have been better to have died an infant, she thought as the weight in her breast became a dull but insistent pain. Or to have been born a bird, or even a fish. Perhaps humans weren't meant for happiness. Even her mother, favored so early by the Moonmaid, had seemed to find little joy in her later life.

Aino had heard the Moonmaid story before: how her needy mother, meeting the moon's daughter in the woods, had pleaded for wedding clothing and been granted her wish. Aino had always wondered why the Moonmaid had never appeared to her mother again. Maybe, she thought now, it only happened once, to a virgin awaiting marriage. If so, would the same spirit be as willing to help Aino as she had her mother? Especially when it was escape Aino wanted? She sent up a prayer to the silver one, and another to her sun-sister as well. *Deliver me.*

At the storehouse, in a small room behind the sacks of grain, barrels of salted fish and wheels of cheese, Aino found a dusty chest. The key fit, and inside, untouched by time, lay a many-layered dress the color of the summer sea. The silky fabric slid like water across Aino's hands as she lifted it out, and when she slipped it over her head it settled like soft ocean waves over her slender curves.

In the bottom of the chest, gold and silver ornaments completed the costume. Aino felt dressed in moonbeams, protected by the Moonmaid's magic. She left the storehouse and walked calmly across the clearing, away from the farm and into the forest.

She knew exactly where to go. The Moonmaid had told her, and she was no longer afraid. Beyond the farthest hill was the ocean, and there she would find her deliverance.

Aino climbed one piney slope and then another. She descended and circled a bog. She walked through a blue woodland haze that rose from the ground and obscured her vision, but her feet went safely over rotted logs, and sharp branches melted away before her. She walked without tiring, with no sense of the hours passing. The noon sun sank unnoticed to evening, and, when she descended the final hill and saw before her the open sea, she was surprised by its darkness and that of the sky.

The black water troubled her, though she knew it was her fate. She thought she would wait until morning, and seated herself upon a stone. Her tears fell softly all through the short night, but the Moonmaid's spirit was with her and her purpose did not waver.

In the light of early morning, Aino saw three maidens bathing far out from shore. They beckoned to her, and she slipped out of her dress. She left it on a bush and her necklace and rings on the pebbly beach, waded into the water and dove into the first wave.

A gleaming rock appeared where the nymphs had been sporting. Aino swam to it, and as she rested there, it sank, bearing her with it to the bottom of the sea.

*   *   *

Aino's mother's lament is still told in the northland:

> "Never again, you poor mothers,
> Never try to trick your daughters
> With your lullabies and rockings
> To accept your choice of husband,
> Wed a man against her will."
>
> *The Kalevala*, Runo 4

*   *   *

It is said that Aino took the form of a salmon, and that Väinämöinen, though he seined the waters with a silken net, was never to able to recapture her. It is also said that every Midsummer Eve a red-haired fisherman leaves the bonfire and the dancing to walk the rocky shore, and that he does not walk alone.

ᔓ ❀ ᘔ

Two

Kylli

Kylli was the island maiden,
Island maiden, island flower.
Brought up in a high-born home . . .
The Kalevala, Runo 11

WON'T YOU AT LEAST TALK TO HIM?" Kylli's mother begged. "He's come such a long way." She held out the silver bracelets. "And such lovely courting gifts. Look at the etchings on these—we have no artists so skilled within a three-day sail."

Kylli handed the bracelets back to her mother. "I'm sorry he wasted so much time and money. But no one told him to come here. No one told any of them. Perhaps this Virolander will carry the word back that I'm not ready to be married, and I'll be left in peace."

Kylli's mother sighed as she tried the silver ornaments on her own wrist, then reached out to smooth one of her daughter's long, wheat-colored braids. "I don't think there's much chance of that. But it wouldn't hurt you to be polite to the young man and give him your refusal in person. We can't afford to make an enemy of Viroland. Your father said—"

Kylli bent her head. "I know. I'll speak to the boy. Tell Father I refused him gently." She started for the room where her suitor waited, but stopped and looked back at her mother with a wry grin. "If only he weren't so short. And with such a big nose!"

The older woman smiled too and shook her head. It wasn't hard for Kylli to guess what she was thinking. *If only her daughter didn't have a stature that dwarfed most men.* Kylli straightened her shoulders and stood proudly at her near six-foot height. It was no problem to her. She could outrun any of her friends on the island, could reach higher with her hay fork and wade deeper with a seining net. Best of all, it made it easier for her to turn away puny suitors.

The Viroland youth took his rejection with good grace. His father had put him up to the journey and the proposal, Kylli suspected. It was the case with most of them who came from over the water. This one was probably relieved to escape from a bold-eyed hoyden who topped him by almost a head.

Be more modest, her mother was continually reminding her. *Lower your eyes and speak softly. Spinning is more seemly than haying or fishing, and kinder to your complexion.*

Kylli only laughed at the advice, but it was becoming more and more difficult for her to go her own carefree way. As a child, growing up with five brothers, she had roamed the island freely, but now she was confined by long skirts and silly prohibitions, and most of all by the necessity of finding a suitable husband.

At least, it wouldn't be this one. "I'll walk with you to your boat," she said to the Virolander. She had admired the sturdy craft from a distance, and here was an opportunity to examine its bright sail and carved prow more closely.

"Not alone, you won't," Kylli's mother objected. She sent a housemaid to accompany the pair, but once outside, Kylli set such a brisk pace that the plump, short-legged chaperone was left far behind.

From the rise of the homestead enclosure, the island estate stretched out in varying shades of brown and green that marked meadows and forests and marshes, all the way to the surrounding, spring-thawed sea. In wooded clearings snow still glistened in patches, but the first warm sunshine was fast melting the remains of winter's breath. Kylli loosened her shawl as she hurried along a muddy trail leading down to the beach and the pier.

The Viroland youth slipped as he struggled to keep up. Kylli reached out to steady him, but he shook off her arm. "Are you always in such a hurry?" he asked. "Or are you so anxious to be rid of me?"

Kylli flushed and proceeded more sedately. Maybe her mother was right; she needed to curb her coltish spirits. "No, I wish you could stay longer," she lied. "I'd like to hear more about your journey."

The latter, at least, was true. Now that the lad was no longer a threat, Kylli felt free to indulge her curiosity about the world beyond the small northern island where she had always lived. "Are there really monstrous fish as big as houses? And serpents that could swallow a boat? How long were you at sea, and were there storms?"

The young man responded as best he could, but before he finished answering one question, Kylli was ready with more. What was it like in Viroland and the regions to the south? What crops did they plant, and how did they build their houses? Was there much war?

Kylli shuddered as she put the last question. It was the one thing she hated about her birthplace—the constant warfare between it and the northern mainland; the raids on both sides for plunder that ended so often in maimings or death. One of her brothers had been lost the previous winter, and another had an arm that hung useless.

Why couldn't the men be satisfied with the bounty of their own fertile lands? Kylli's father's estate comprised almost the whole of one island in the archipelago, and his family and tenants never wanted for game or fish. His cows were fat, even in winter, and no women on the island had been driven to bake famine bread.

Yes, there were wars in Viroland, the young man said. Raiders came from Kaleva, and sometimes even from Ingerland. He squared his shoulders and made fists of his hands. "We have a score to settle with a certain tribe in Ingerland, and I'm to go along when we do it." He drew an imaginary sword and waved it about in wide slashes. "I've been practicing—with the crossbow, too—and Father says I'm ready. Maybe—" He took a step closer to Kylli and peered up into her face. "Maybe I can bring you some plunder. Ingerland gold. Would it make you look kinder on me?"

Kylli sighed as she shook her head. "No, the answer I gave you is final." Why couldn't any of them understand that she wasn't to be won by bragging speeches or promises of ill-gotten riches? The one thing she knew for a certainty about her future mate was that he would *not* be a warrior. She regarded her suitor with ill-concealed disdain. Nor would he be an undersized, beardless lad. She continued down the trail, walking fast again, not interested in further conversation.

When they reached the harbor, they found the Viroland crew waiting by the boat. Kylli no longer felt like inspecting it, and she bade the travelers a final farewell from the beach.

As she started back up the trail, Kylli met Senja, the housemaid, coming down. Kylli motioned for her to turn around and retrace her steps, but the red-faced, panting girl collapsed on a tree stump. "Please, can't we rest a few minutes?" she begged. "I'll never make it back, otherwise." She looked longingly up a branching path that led to a nearby tenant farmer's hut. "Couldn't we stop off a while at the Kauppis? Your mother wouldn't mind, I'm sure."

"Why not?" Kylli agreed. A cool drink would be welcome, as well as a gossip with Inkeri, Kauppi's daughter.

Senja leaped up from the stump and started up the new path with renewed energy. Kylli followed almost as eagerly. Inkeri, though far below her in social station, was nevertheless her closest friend. Kylli was prepared for the teasing she would receive about her latest suitor, and already had a tart rejoinder ready. She smiled in anticipation.

The Kauppis' log hut nestled in a small clearing shaded by surrounding pines. Inkeri waved to her visitors from the doorstep, where she sat knitting a bright green scarf. The tenant farmer's daughter was small and dark, a striking contrast to Kylli, with narrow, laughing eyes that disappeared into folds at the outer corners. A yoke with two water buckets lay on the ground beside her, and as Kylli and Senja approached she hastily put aside her knitting and hefted the empty containers. "Come with me to the well," she said. "I'm supposed to be fetching water for Mama. She'll be yelling for it in a minute, but I wanted to get that scarf finished by tonight." She giggled. "You'll never guess who it's for."

"I know already," Senja said as they started for the wellhouse. "It's the new herd boy, isn't it?"

Inkeri colored. "Well, I guess it's no secret. You must have seen me showing him where to take the cows." She turned to Kylli. "Have you seen him yet?"

"No, I haven't," Kylli said somewhat crossly. Her own affairs seemed to be of no importance. A herd boy, indeed! "I didn't know Father had even hired someone."

They were at the well, and Kylli helped her friend lower and raise the buckets. "Here, let me carry them," she said, lifting the yoke to her own broad shoulders. Inkeri would end up slopping water on her skirts, and Kylli had no wish to hear the scolding she would receive.

Back at the cabin, Kylli deposited the buckets inside the door, and the three girls fled down the trail before Inkeri's mother could assign her daughter more tasks. The old woman had a deserved reputation as a shrew, and Kylli was as anxious as the others to escape her sharp eyes and tongue.

They stopped in a grove of white-trunked birches and found seats on a mossy log. Inkeri took out her knitting again and returned to the subject of the new herd boy. "His name is Lemminkäinen, and he comes from the mainland, out by Cape Far."

"That's a bit of a journey," Kylli said. "What's he doing here?"

Senja answered, with a wink. "Looking over the island girls, I expect. I met him, too. He's real . . . flirty."

"He *is* friendly," Inkeri agreed. She turned an inquiring gaze on Kylli. "You really haven't heard about him?"

"No, we've had a guest at the house," Kylli said. "A Virolander." She prepared herself for a rush of questions.

Inkeri, however, displayed no interest. "Well, wait until you see this new fellow," she said. "He's wonderfully handsome—tall, well built, with black hair and a curly black beard. He's a great talker, too. His stories . . . I don't know when I've laughed so hard. And those eyes. . . . "

Kylli refused to be impressed. "So what is this superior example of manhood doing herding cows?"

Inkeri frowned. "I'm not sure. Actually, he's years too old to be a herd boy."

"Or too young," Senja added, and Kylli nodded. Cattle tenders on the island were usually either stripling youths or doddering old men.

Inkeri continued: "I suppose he's poor and needs the job. His clothes are really shabby." She held up the knitting. "That's why I'm making him this. Kind of a welcoming present."

"I hope he deserves it," Kylli said.

"I don't know about that." A crimson blush again stained Inkeri's cheeks. "I only know that he's . . . awfully nice. And I think he likes me."

Kylli gave her friend a hug. Inkeri fell in love too easily, and was too easily hurt. It had happened often enough that Kylli could foresee the tears. Whoever this Lemminkäinen was, he'd better watch his step.

* * *

Kylli met the new herd boy the next morning, as he was leading the animals out to pasture. She had stationed herself beside the barnyard gate for that purpose, and he did not seem surprised to see her there. "You must be Kyllikki," he said. "The famous Kyllikki. The renowned island beauty."

She didn't like his insolent tone, or his use of the affectionate suffix. "Kylli to you," she said. He was, she granted, as handsome as Inkeri had described, but that was all she could put to his favor. His clothing was indeed shabby, his jerkin doubly patched and his birch bark shoes about ready to fall apart.

He made her a mocking bow. "Mistress Kylli. Perhaps you would care to accompany me a ways. Show me the best grasses and warn me of the marshes." He jiggled the knapsack on his shoulder. "Perhaps share lunch with me in one of your father's forest glades."

How dare he! Kylli straightened her shoulders and glared at him. "I believe Inkeri has already shown you all that is necessary." And probably shared the forest glade, too. She noted with displeasure that he was wearing the green scarf.

"As you wish." He touched his cap, but he didn't doff it. "Until this evening, then." He followed the last cow through the gate, leaving her to close it.

She did, fuming at his impudence, his lack of respect. What did he mean by "this evening?" Did he expect to sit around the stove at night, with the family? Although young people from the estate sometimes gathered there in the big room, with their sewing and mending and carving, she hardly thought that a herd boy. . . .

He was unusual, though. Taller even than her father. And muscular, too, she could tell even through his clothing. The breadth of those shoulders. . . . She climbed the gate to view him better as he strode across the pasture, and, when he turned and caught her staring, she suffered a flood of embarrassment.

She strode away angrily, back to the barn where her father and the two farm workers were harnessing plows to horses. She longed to work the fields with them, but, though she could plow a furrow as straight as any man, she didn't expect her father to allow her the opportunity.

She was right. "Your mother wants you at the house," he said before she could open her mouth.

Weaving, she thought, wrinkling her nose. Long, tedious hours with the loom and shuttle. Imprisonment.

Inside the house, Kylli's mother shook her head at her daughter's long face. "You can do the baking, if you'd rather," she offered, but Kylli took her place at the loom. Cooking was less restricting, but she didn't appreciate the comments that always arose from her lumpy loaves and burnt cakes. Plying the shuttle, at least her mind could roam free.

Senja was off in the grinding shed, and Kylli and her mother worked alone in the big central room of the manor house. It had rugs on the polished white birch floor, padded benches, a stove with a chimney instead of a fire pit and smoke hole like the tenant huts, and private closets for sleeping. Kylli knew well that she was fortunate in her position. If she didn't, her mother was constantly reminding her. "The Virolander wouldn't have been a bad match," she said now as she mixed dough for wheat cakes. "But don't worry, there'll be others. Not so many, perhaps—after all, you're not as young any more as some suiters might wish—but still, no need to settle for less than we have here."

I'm only nineteen, Kylli wanted to protest, but she held her tongue. Her mother had had two children by that age. Kylli was being warned, she knew, not to wait too long.

Why couldn't she be more content, she thought as the cords of her loom hummed. More like other women. She knew she was the envy of Senja and Inkeri and the other unmarried girls on the island. She could pick and choose among noble suitors, could look forward to a life of comparative ease. There would be no hasty marriage for her, no seven-month baby and no smoky hut and sullen husband and crabbing mother-in-law.

Why, then, did her thoughts dwell with something suspiciously like jealousy on Inkeri and her foolish infatuation? It would probably come to nothing, and if it didn't, what kind of a life could her friend expect with a penniless rogue like Lemminkäinen?

Kylli fretted all through the day, and that night when she saw the new couple together it made her feel worse than ever. An impromptu party had developed from the after-work gathering of young people at the manor house. Hannu the fisherman brought out his harp, and Lemminkäinen was the most eager of the dancers. Kylli watched from the high bench, observing with distress Inkeri's woeful face whenever the newcomer partnered someone else, and there wasn't a maiden in the room who wasn't twirled in his strong arms.

Except Kylli herself, who remained aloof and did not dance at all. She refused Lemminkäinen three times, and no one else had the boldness to ask her. When the party broke up, Inkeri left with Lemminkäinen, but her firm grip on his arm did not prevent him from smiling at every other young woman on their way out.

Kylli did not sleep well that night. She told herself that she should warn Inkeri, but what could she say that her friend wouldn't resent? Still, she had to do something. . . .

The next morning, Kylli was again at the gate, and again the cattle tender did not appear surprised. "A good morning, Mistress Kylli," he said politely, but the look in his eyes was far too admiring to be properly respectful.

Kylli ignored the look, but she couldn't help being glad that she had coiled her braids becomingly over her ears. "I came to speak to you about Inkeri," she said, making her voice as stern as that of the most severe taskmaster. "You should know that she is under my family's protection, and if she is ill used. . . . "

"Ill used." Lemminkäinen smiled at the words. "I'm not sure I know what you mean."

"I think you do," she replied.

"Perhaps you should ask her whether she considers it ill." His eyes mocked her.

She refused to let his manner distract her. "Are your intentions honorable?"

"I have no intentions at all," he answered. "Except towards you, dear Mistress, and they are indeed honorable. But since you wouldn't even dance with me—"

"Dance with you!" Kylli gasped as confusion overcame her. "Intentions! Surely you can't mean—not you and me!"

He came closer to her, leaning on the fence that separated them. "We would make a perfect pair, wouldn't we? It's the reason I came to the island, to see whether you justified your fame. And aside from a certain lack of warmth in your manner, I can't say I'm disappointed."

Speechless, Kylli withdrew a pace, then turned her back and fled.

18

"I'll be waiting for your answer," he called after her. She didn't think he was laughing, but she couldn't be sure.

Kylli spent the day at the house of one of her married brothers and, with little persuasion, spent the night, too. Listening to a squalling baby was better than facing the impudent cow herder, and the longer she could put it off the better.

Did he actually expect her to take his proposal seriously? It was too ridiculous. Surely he must realize that her father would have him expelled from the island. He wasn't the first threadbare fortune-hunter to come, but perhaps he considered his physical charms protection against the swift fate of the others.

If so, he was due for a surprise. Kylli had her bitterly worded rejection speech ready when she finally returned home, to find Inkeri waiting for her with a tear-stained face.

"It's all over," Inkeri sobbed. "Last night he went walking with the widow Kuusi. Senja saw them. I waited for him until after midnight, and this morning he acted like . . . like there had been nothing between us."

"And had there been? Did he make you any promises?" Kylli asked as she patted her friend's heaving shoulders.

"No, not exactly. But I thought . . . I hoped . . . that he loved me, too." Inkeri collapsed again into tears.

Kylli mentally added a few more choice phrases to her speech. She saw Inkeri home and spent most of the day with her. That night the young people gathered at the widow Kuusi's, but neither Inkeri nor Kylli went. Inkeri, of course, was too heartbroken, and Kylli was too loyal. Kylli felt a bit rebuffed, herself, and doubted now that her well-rehearsed speech would ever be needed.

Kylli didn't see Lemminkäinen for several days, but Senja reported that he spent his evenings at the widow's. When she next encountered him, while she was berrying with her two small nieces, Kylli nodded coldly but did not speak. The children ran up to one of the cows, and before she could call them back the herder was accepting berries in return for screaming rides on his shoulders.

"At least some of the women in your family like me," he said as he returned the giggling girls.

"They aren't women," Kylli said. "Perhaps when they are, they'll have more judgment."

"You sound annoyed. More than usual, that is. I had hoped for kinder words."

"Kinder!" Her voice broke on a squeak. What in Ukko's realm did he expect? "After the unprincipled way you've been behaving? First poor

Inkeri, now the Kuusi woman, who's barely buried her husband. What kind of a game are you playing?"

He answered calmly, his steady gaze maddeningly disconcerting. "Yes, it's all a game. Just to amuse myself while I'm waiting for your answer. Have you forgotten? I'm still waiting."

Her rehearsed speech flew out of her mind. "Hooligan!" she hissed. "Do you think I'd ever marry such a one as you? No! My answer is no! And you'd better get any such ideas out of your head before my father or brothers find out. You'd be sorry then, I can assure you of that."

"I'm sorry now," he said. "But I'm also patient, and I have hopes that you'll change your mind. I'll bide my time and ask you again."

Lemminkäinen did ask her, whenever they met, in the weeks that followed. Kylli tried to avoid him, but it was impossible when he was at every summer frolic. He was the most agile dancer, the winner in every footrace, a stronger rower than her own brothers, and undisputably the handsomest man who had ever graced the island. Kylli's constant refusals did not seem to dampen his spirits, especially when he had no lack of other young women with whom to console himself. Kylli fumed inwardly every time she heard of a new conquest, and though she told herself repeatedly that it should mean nothing to her, she couldn't help listening jealously to Senja's gossip.

A word to her father would have rid her easily of the annoyance, but she did not speak the word. Instead, as summer blossomed and the days grew long and warm, she took to solitary evening walks that ended often at the seashore. Gazing out at the waves, more than ever before she felt dissatisfied with her circumscribed life. Other longings that she didn't understand filled her as well; ones that made her flee from Lemminkäinen yet not wish him to leave the island.

One such evening, heading for a distant cove, she stopped in a forest glade where Inkeri and several of her other friends were enjoying the late sunlight and soft grass with singing and barefoot dancing. Kylli had barely slipped off her own shoes to join them when a horse and sleigh burst into the clearing.

It was Lemminkäinen, and while the other girls shrieked, he swooped up Kylli and deposited her face down on the bearskin. Urging the horse ahead at full gallop, he shouted back threats not to raise an alarm. Kylli struggled to free herself, but they were going too fast and Lemminkäinen's grip on her was too strong. She wept and pleaded, but to no avail; their pace did not slacken until they were through the forest and well out of reach of pursuit.

There would be a boat hidden on a beach, Kylli suspected, and they would be at sea before dark. She had heard of kidnapped brides—there was even one on the island—but she had never dreamed it would happen to her.

If that was what he intended—and why else take such a risk?—he was a dead man. "My brothers will kill you," she said into the bearskin.

"If you allow it." He loosened his grip enough for her to sit, but kept one arm pinioning her in place. "Not if you send word that you are content."

He silenced her protest. "Please. You are not to worry. I'm not exactly taking you to a life of poverty. My Kyllikki." His voice caressed the words as his hand caressed her arm, and though she could now have broken free, she did not do so. "I have a small farm," he continued. "Nothing, of course, like your father's. My three cows don't need a herd boy, and I can plow my fields myself. You will never be hungry, though, or lonely, or cold at night." His arm pressed her closer, and again she did not object. She was suddenly tired of protesting, of denying, of pretending. To be relieved of decision—and with such a one as Lemminkäinen—it was almost a blessing. Nor was she afraid of poverty. At the very least, there would be no more embroidering linens.

Lemminkäinen continued: "I know that my family isn't noble, and my homestead isn't what you're used to, but I have a good sword and I know how to use it. There are lots of opportunities for a warrior of my talents, lots of gold and silver to be won, and with you to inspire me, I can promise we won't be humble dirt farmers for long."

A warrior! Kylli stiffened and jerked herself away from him. Just when she was beginning to weaken, to have him turn out like all the others! "That's one promise I don't want," she said through clenched teeth.

"What's wrong?" He stopped the horse and took her gently into his arms. "Just tell me. I'll promise you anything if it will make you love me."

"I think I already do," she said. "But I won't go with you willingly unless you swear never to go to war. I've seen too much of its results. I'd rather be poor, and have you safe, than suffer the torments of a waiting wife."

"Is that all?" he said, laughing. "I can swear to that easily." He raised his right arm to the sky. "Hear me, Ukko, that never, even for the direst lack of goods, will I leave my wife to go warring." He turned to Kylli. "Now you. Your promise."

"What is it?" she asked, a bit nervously. "What must I pledge?"

"Only that you will be a faithful, homebound wife. One who won't gad about the village and join the other gossips at their parties." He glanced at her feet. "No more dancing barefoot in the forest."

Was that all? Kylli breathed a sigh of relief. As a farm wife, she knew she would have little time for such frivolities. She gave her promise gladly, then allowed herself to sink down into Lemminkäinen's waiting arms.

* * *

Then that Ahti, Lemminkäinen,
He the handsome man far-minded,
For a time lived pleasantly
With his young bride by his side;
He did not go off to war

The Kalevala, Runo 12

* * *

Lemminkäinen's homestead was both better and worse than Kylli had expected. The house was a log hut with a smokehole, ill-furnished and none too clean, and contained a resident mother-in-law. However, it was sturdy and well-chinked, the roof tightly covered with birch bark, and the mother-in-law was good natured—delighted with Kylli and content to sit in a corner spinning while the younger woman took over the cooking and cleaning and washing. The farm was still mostly in woods, with a single cleared pasture and an uncut hay field. The old mother had a weedy potato patch and some scrawny pigs that rooted in a pen much too near the house, but the three cows were sleek and fat and the barn did not leak.

Kylli gave herself up to her new life as eagerly as she went at night into Lemminkäinen's arms. The housework she accomplished easily, with ample time to help Lemminkäinen in the fields. The house soon shone, the hay was stacked in the barn, a new field was cleared and burned, and the happy couple could gaze with pride on their well-ordered home.

Kylli didn't mind eating coarse rye bread instead of soft wheat, she didn't mind covering her braids with a matronly kerchief, and she didn't even—at first—miss her friends and family. For two fortnights Lemminkäinen scarcely left her side, and he was so kind and loving that she had no desire for other company.

It was in the fifth week, when Lemminkäinen had driven the sleigh to a neighbor's to look at a horse, that Kylli first felt the loneliness of the isolated farm. The old mother was not disposed to conversation, and outside, an autumn rain darkened the sky. The wooded hills that encircled the cabin seemed to Kylli that day like the walls of a prison. She wasted most of the afternoon at the window, staring down the trail, but her will could not make the sleigh appear. Blackie and Crannie and Strawberry lowed mournfully to be let into the barn, and when the two women went to their milking, Lemminkäinen still had not returned. The mother wasn't troubled. "They'll be toasting my boy's wedding," she said with a cackle, but Kylli gritted her teeth and wondered why she should be left out of the celebration.

Lemminkäinen returned after dark, with beer on his breath and a thick head. Kylli would have spoken sharp words if the mother-in-law hadn't been present, but as it was she let her resentment smolder.

The next time Lemminkäinen harnessed the sleigh, for a trip to the nearest village, Kylli asked to go along.

She did not expect his frowning response. "Of course not," he snapped. "Your place is here, with my mother. Have you forgotten your pledge?"

For a moment she was puzzled. "Oh, that," she said, remembering. "Not to go gadding about. I hardly think a trip with my husband qualifies."

"It certainly does," Lemminkäinen replied. "I have my own business to attend to, and I can't be with you every minute. I don't want you going alone into people's houses."

Kylli set her mouth as sternly as his. "How silly! Am I never to meet our neighbors? Perhaps you're ashamed of me. Is that the reason? Now that I wear an apron and cover my hair, have I suddenly grown ugly?"

He didn't answer, but leaped into the sleigh. "Your place is here," he repeated before driving off.

Kylli blinked away tears. She didn't dare to complain to Lemminkäinen's mother, who would surely have taken her son's side, so once more she kept her grievance to herself. She didn't think she was being overly reactive: her brothers' wives had always visited about freely on the island. She had never considered Lemminkäinen to be the jealous type, and she began to wonder if it was he who had something to hide. A mistress, perhaps. Or merely gossip she wasn't supposed to hear.

She worked furiously outside all day, digging holes and pounding in posts for a new fence. When Lemminkäinen returned, again very late, she set his supper before him without a word.

He pushed away the plate. "I've eaten," he said.

"Where?" She folded her arms and waited.

He merely shrugged. The old mother looked up from her sewing with a shake of her head and a "tsk, tsk," and he slammed out of the house.

They made up their quarrel without words that night on the straw pallet, but though Lemminkäinen made no more trips to the village, to Kylli her marriage had lost some of its luster. She no longer trusted her husband completely, and for all Lemminkäinen's good looks and his skill at lovemaking, she yearned for other companionship. If only she could have unburdened herself to Inkeri! If only she could laugh and tease and gossip again with her brothers' wives and her friends! Working in the fields and forest afforded her some relief, but even there she began to sense that Lemminkäinen did not appreciate the ease with which she matched and sometimes even surpassed his efforts with the axe and shovel. She persisted, however—why should she play a part just to pamper a foolish ego?—until the first snow fell and the outdoor freedom was closed to her. Then, the cabin shrank in size until she could almost feel its smoky walls pressing in on her.

They were well-provisioned for winter, but Lemminkäinen wanted one more catch of fish for salting. Kylli had gone with him before, but this time he refused even to consider it. "I'll be back by noon," he said. "I'll only fish from shore, so I won't need your help with the boat." The fishing grounds were not far and the day was clear, so there was no reason he could not keep his promise. Whatever doubts she had, Kylli kept to herself.

He didn't return by noon, or even by dark. If there had been a storm, Kylli would have worried, but lying alone that night she only grew increasingly angry.

In the morning, she wrapped herself well in furs and strapped on her skis. "Don't go," the mother-in-law begged. "He's fine, I'm sure. He's probably visiting at a friend's house, and he'll be annoyed that you went looking for him."

"Then I'm going visiting, too," Kylli said. "If you think he'll be upset, you don't need to tell him."

The old woman was still protesting when Kylli started off. The trail to the village was well-covered with fresh snow under a hard crust, the skiing was easy, and Kylli arrived at the first house within an hour.

A mother and daughter welcomed her warmly. "No, we haven't seen Lemminkäinen," they said. "But he's probably still at Tiera's house. The men had quite a party there last night, from all the shouting we heard."

"Yes, of course," Kylli said, pretending she knew all about it. Tiera, she had heard from her mother-in-law, was an old raiding and plundering companion of Lemminkäinen's, one whom she had hoped belonged only to his former life.

"Now we can have our own party," the older woman, Sinikka, said. "We've been waiting to meet the new bride." She sent her daughter to spread the word among the neighbors, and within another hour a group of women was gathered around Sinikka's hearth.

Food came out—fish roe and bread and cream cakes—and Kylli enjoyed the pleasantest morning she had spent in weeks. She made new friends and learned the village gossip, much of which concerned Lemminkäinen and the hearts he had broken. Some of the women looked at Kylli askance when certain names were mentioned, but she only laughed. Knowing how Lemminkäinen had behaved on the island, it did not surprise her that he had sowed wild oats here as well.

"We always knew he would some day bring home the finest bride," Sinikka said. She had Kylli stand while the others exclaimed over her stature and beauty and apparent strength. "We knew it would take someone like you to tame him."

If he were tamed, Kylli thought. None of the gossip was recent, which afforded her a measure of ease, though she doubted that any new scandal about her husband would be repeated in her presence. She responded good-naturedly to the inevitable teasing, invited the women to visit (wondering only fleetingly what Lemminkäinen would say), and left the village much lighter of heart than she had entered it.

If only Lemminkäinen were still away, she thought as she skied home. And if only his mother would hold her tongue. She didn't feel guilty about her innocent morning, but knowing Lemminkäinen as she did, she could only expect an unpleasant scene if he found out.

Her heart fell as she came out of the forest and saw the sleigh beside the barn. Still, she reminded herself, she had no reason to be ashamed. She left her skis by the door and held her head high as she entered the house.

Lemminkäinen sat by the fireplace, polishing the mail of his battle armor, and his mother crouched in her corner, weeping. Both pairs of eyes fastened on Kylli.

The mother spoke first. "Tell him he mustn't go," she wailed. "Tell him we don't need gold from Pohjola, that we have furs and food enough here. Tell him not to go to that dark, evil place." She turned to her son. "They'll work their magic tricks on you, and you won't be able to counter them." She broke into fresh weeping. "And alone—you'll never return!"

"Stop it, Mother," Lemminkäinen said. "Why should I be afraid of Northland magic? My sword and bow will answer it well enough. And I won't be alone. I'll get Tiera to go with me, and there'll be other men from the village eager for adventure."

Kylli, still dressed in her furs, stared at him without moving. "So you're going," she said. Her heart was a dead weight. "What about the promise you made me? I suppose it means nothing."

He stared back. "Not any longer. Not since you broke yours, and released me. Not since you dishonored me."

"Dishonored you?" Her voice rose. "By eating fish eggs with some village women? Where's the dishonor there?"

Lemminkäinen's face remained impassive. "How do I know there were only women there? Old Sinikka has a son, too."

"Well, he wasn't at home!" Furiously, Kylli unfastened her furs and threw them aside. The house was as hot as a sauna. "If you don't believe me, why don't you go over there and ask them?"

"I would never do that," he said stiffly.

"Then I guess you'll never know, will you." She sat down abruptly at the table, her chin in her hands, staring at the wall.

"I know quite enough," he said. "I know that you've broken your pledge, and because of it I'm no longer bound to you. I'm free to go when and where I please, and that's exactly what I intend to do."

Lemminkäinen resumed his polishing, until the mail gleamed. The old woman continued to weep, and Kylli to stare at the wall. He had planned it all, she suspected. From the very beginning. The silly pledge, knowing full well she wouldn't keep it. Putting her in the wrong so he could resume his warring, bachelor life.

They passed a silent, tense afternoon. Lemminkäinen completed his preparations for leaving, made a trip to the village and returned with news of a willing war party, and there appeared nothing the two women could do to prevent his departure. The mother made a last attempt, after a supper which he alone had enjoyed. "What if you're gone all winter?" She whined pitiably and squeezed her hands. "What if we run out of meat, with no one to go hunting? Have you even thought what might become of us, two women alone?"

Lemminkäinen sheathed the sword he had been whetting. "You don't need me," he said with a shrug. "Kyllikki, I'm sure, can hunt and trap as well as any man." He turned to her, where she stood washing the supper bowls. "Can't you, my sweet?"

There was no affection in his voice, or in the look he gave her, and Kylli shivered. "I don't like killing," she said. "Even animals."

"Then you wouldn't make a warrior." His voice was even colder. "At least it's one way you won't try to better me."

She opened her mouth to protest—was that what he had been thinking about her?—but decided he was in no mood to listen.

He had certainly succeeded in all his plans. But what if I'm not here when you return? she wanted to say, but again she remained silent. He knew she had nowhere to go, that she was far too proud to return to her father's house, even if he would take her in, and that no one else would do so. She would be here to greet the returned plunderer warmly, because by then she would be lonely enough to forgive anything. She would bind up his wounds, nurse him and probably love him again, only to have it all repeated the next time he thirsted for adventure.

She finished her chores quickly and prepared for bed. It was too early to sleep, but she couldn't bear to sit and watch Lemminkäinen do his final packing. She lay rigidly on the straw behind their curtain, locked in misery, as she heard him go in and out of the house, presumably loading his sleigh for an early departure.

After an hour or so the commotion ceased. When Lemminkäinen parted the curtain and looked in on her, Kylli pretended to be asleep. After all that had been said, would he expect her to open her arms to him?

But he made no move to join her. She heard him murmur something to his mother, then the mother's sharp cry and shocked reply.

"Another bride!" The old woman made no attempt to keep her voice low. "How can you even think of such a thing, when you already have Kyllikki? Yes, I've heard about those northern girls, and how beautiful they're supposed to be, but I don't believe a word of it. Witches, that's what they are up there. All of them. You'll be sorry if you bring one back. That is, if you live to do it." She subsided into muttering, then broke out again. "Two wives in one bed!" Kylli could imagine her throwing up her hands. "It would be a scandal!"

"No, no, it wouldn't be like that." Now Lemminkäinen had forgotten, too, to whisper. "I'll bind out Kylli to one of the neighbors." His voice turned bitter. "She seems to like them so much, it ought to suit her fine."

"*Voi, voi,*" the mother muttered. "It will turn out badly, I've dreamed the signs. If you go, you'll surely meet your ruin."

Lemminkäinen barked an oath and there was a thudding sound, as of small objects hurled against the wall, then his growling rejoinder. "Why must you see doom in everything? Come to ruin? Why, that comb and brush will begin to bleed before anything happens to me. Now, if you can't wish me well—"

"You know I do," came the mother's tremulous reply. "If you must go, then come here, and let me do what I can." There was a shuffling, followed by the old woman's voice in a tuneless chant. Kylli could catch few of the words, but she recognized it as a charm against danger in war, addressed both to Ukko, the old god, and to Jumala, the new.

If only there were a charm to protect her, Kylli thought as she curled into a tight ball. To be bound out almost as a slave! He had the right, she knew, and even her father could not interfere.

She cast about desperately for options. There was a woman on the island who had fled from an abusively evil husband, who barely subsisted as a wandering drudge. But Kylli, if she left Lemminkäinen now, couldn't even claim that kind of mistreatment. She shuddered to think of the life she might lead, with all respectable doors closed to her.

But to remain, and see her husband come home with a new bride! To be supplanted but not freed!

If only she were a man, she could make her way easily anywhere. She could fish, or do farm work, or herd reindeer in the north. She could sail to one of the far southern lands where there were said to be great cities and endless opportunities. Beholden to no one, she could wander freely and satisfy her own thirst for adventure.

If only . . . she thought. And then . . . why not? If Lemminkäinen despised her for her manly skills, why not use them for her own benefit? For her escape. With her stature and broad shoulders, she could easily pass as a man. Or at least, as a beardless youth.

She hugged herself in her excitement, planning how she would cut her hair and dress in Lemminkäinen's old, patched clothing, how she would ski to the south and make her way from village to village. She would be a younger son out to earn his own fortune, willing to try his hand at any honest work. She would see all the places she had ever wondered about, and never, ever, would she again have to sit at a loom or scrub someone else's dirty breeches.

Lemminkäinen spent the night on the stove bench, and when Kylli finally fell asleep, she dreamed of the next morning, when he would be gone. In the dream, the mother sat by the dead fire, still weeping. She scarcely noticed when Kylli dressed herself as a man, only rousing herself to say that Kylli was wise to leave before—and here she broke into fresh wailing—before her son returned with a witch wife.

"You mustn't worry about me," the old woman said when she had somewhat recovered. "I've weathered winters here before, waiting for my boy. Maybe this time he'll be sorry, when he returns and finds you gone."

"No, he'll be glad to be rid of me," Kylli said as in her dream she hacked off her braid with the skinning knife. *And me him,* she wanted to add, but she knew it wouldn't be quite true. There had been moments. . . . Enough that she couldn't bear to look backwards when she skied into the forest, but not enough to extinguish the spark of joy that burned in her when she thought of what lay ahead.

When she awoke, Kylli immediately felt for her braid, and when she found it intact she could have wept with disappointment. Would she have the courage, in the cold light of day? She parted the curtain and saw that Lemminkäinen was gone. His mother sat by the dead fire, staring fixidly at the comb and brush on the floor.

Kylli shivered. *This is no dream,* she thought, and desperately sought to recapture her resolution of the night before. *This is my life.*

* * *

It was told by the early singers, all of them men, that Kylli, the "lovely housewife," waited loyally for Lemminkäinen's return. One who came later, however, says that a boyish figure resembling the runaway wife was seen in Kaleva and in Viroland and even farther to the south, but since no one recognized her it can never be proven.

ༀ ❀ ౧

Three

Lahja the Maiden

ಬ ❀ ಬ

Oh! she was fair, that northern maiden,
Famed afar on land and sea . . .
The Kalevala, Runo 8

T hey called her the witch's daughter, and had she been less beautiful she would have shared in the hatred the Kalevalanders directed at her mother. But as it was, Lahja from the age of twelve had had no lack of suitors, inspiring jealousy in her older sisters and avarice in the heart of her witch parent. Her father, Taisto, who doted on her, would have kept her hidden safely at home, but though he was nominally the master of North Farm it was his wife, Louhi, who really ruled there as well as in all the tribal lands of Pohjola.

Louhi was an imposing woman: tall and black-haired, with an air of authority few dared to challenge. Lahja, as far back as she could remember, had been afraid of her. Not that in their tender years she or her sisters had seen their mother often, for Louhi had more important duties than the care of small children. Lahja's nursemaid had warned her never to annoy the mistress, and, from the first time she had seen Louhi angry, her usually calm, proud face transformed into a mask of fury, Lahja had heeded the warning and kept her distance.

It wasn't difficult, for Louhi was seldom home. There were tribal councils to be presided over, disputes to be settled, and always the scavenging raiders from southern and eastern lands to be driven off. Lahja's small, fair-haired father, who was no warrior, contentedly worked the farm, but it was Louhi who kept them supplied with slaves, who drove off wolves with magic chants, and who even in the worst years kept them better fed than their neighbors.

When she was eight, Lahja first witnessed her mother's full powers. Taisto had driven his sleigh to a hill at the farm's border, to see his wife off on one of her skirmishes against the Kalevalanders. Lahja had crawled under a bearskin in the rear of the sleigh, planning to remain hidden until the ride home. When the sleigh stopped and she was sure her mother was gone, Lahja peered out to see the fierce woman in battle armor harangue her ragged warriors. She watched, frightened but fascinated, as Louhi raised her arms and chanted an incantation, then gasped with terror as the mailed figure transformed herself into a fiery-taloned eagle who screamed a savage war cry as she took to the air.

Lahja closed her eyes tightly and screamed, too.

"Child!" Taisto turned and pulled her out of the nest of furs. "It's all right, it's all right," he repeated as he held her. "It's just a trick, to scare the enemy. Look"—he pried her face away from his chest—"look and you'll see. There she is, the same as always."

Lahja opened her eyes, and the eagle was gone. Her mother marched down the hill at the head of the line of men, and soon they disappeared into a forest. "The same as always," her father repeated.

To Lahja, however, her mother was never again the same. Though her father repeatedly reassured her that Louhi would only use her powers to protect the family, the farm, and Pohjola, in the child's mind the fiery eagle always lurked beneath her mother's human appearance. She remembered every word of the incantation that had produced the transformation; a dark secret that she would rather have forgotten.

Lahja never knew whether the eagle had appeared in that particular battle, or in others that followed, but, whatever the reason, the Pohjolanders usually came home victorious.

Unfortunately, the few spoils did not go far. "If only she could make corn or wheat grow in our fields," Lahja's plump sister Kaisa, who loved to eat but hated barley-cakes, often complained.

"Or get us new dresses," the oldest sister, Toini, would add. Toini had a distressingly long, sharp nose, loved finery, and, with only two homespun dresses in her clothes chest, wore a habitually cross expression.

Lahja had a small appetite and was too young to worry about her appearance, but she couldn't help but notice the increasing numbers of poor and hungry who came to the North Farm storehouse door. Louhi, for all her successes in war, could do little to relieve the poverty of her domain. Pohjola was a country of dark forests and frozen seas, of long, cold winters when a single sack of rye or barley stood between a family and starvation.

When Lahja was ten, a blight destroyed the summer grains. In the winter of her eleventh year, most of the reindeer were lost in a blizzard and the remainder found scant moss on which to feed. Beggars went home empty-handed, and though Louhi secreted herself for days at a time in a mountain cave, whatever magic she sought to work could not break the famine.

At North Farm they still had rye for bread, but elsewhere the peasants ate loaves baked with pine bark and marshland grasses. Louhi had her slaves carry armloads of wood into her cave, then a heavy cask from her treasure room. Columns of smoke issued from the cave's mouth, then tongues of flame, but Louhi returned home from each new attempt at fiery witchcraft with a soot-smeared face and blistered, empty hands.

"A Sampo," Lahja heard her explain at night to Taisto, their voices carrying from their bed across the long, plank-floored room. "A magic mill. No one in Pohjola would ever be hungry again. I could make it work—make it run forever. I feel the power, and I know the charms. I know exactly how it should look. Even in the dark I can see it—the very inscriptions on its cover—but"—a howl of anguish caused the listening girls to huddle together on their pallet—"I can't fashion it, no matter how I try. I'm no blacksmith, and there's no one else here who has the skill."

A magic mill. Lahja could see it, too, glowing in the darkness, its spinning cover grinding out an inexhaustible stream of the finest grain. "If you only could," came her father's answering voice, then her mother's again, this time in a low murmur. Lahja could distinguish few of the words, only her name, "Lahja," and "it's the only way," repeated several times.

Though hard times continued in Pohjola, Louhi somehow continued to find food for her family. The choicest portions—the fattest pieces of meat and the occasional bit of butter—she allotted to Lahja, who, in spite of her sisters' dark looks, was both too hungry and too frightened of her mother to refuse. The dark looks turned to secret pinches and hair-pullings when Louhi produced a foreign-made dress of watered silk for Lahja to wear whenever there were guests at the house, and again Lahja had no choice but to play the obedient daughter.

At twelve, Lahja's exceptional loveliness was legendary. Her hair was as black as Louhi's, but whereas the witch's was dark and coarse under her headcloth, Lahja's was glossy and soft as a skein of silk. Her blue eyes she inherited from her father: remarkable soul-mirrors which could reflect any shade between the dawn-blue of cornflowers and the dusk-blue of a winter sunset. Her delicate features and sweetly rounded face aroused tender feelings in the most hardened male heart; feelings that Louhi knew well how to use to advantage.

Youths from both Pohjola and Kaleva came to stare, and older men to make offers of pigs and horses and hoarded furs. None of them, however, could make a Sampo, and Louhi dismissed them without ceremony. Lahja shrank inside whenever she had to put on the dress and smile. It didn't help that Kaisa and Toini made fun of every prospective suitor—this one had bad teeth, and that one smelled like a stable—and called her an auctioned calf.

It was exactly the way she felt about herself. Shame mingled with fear of what lay ahead if her mother should actually approve of one of the suitors. For a whole year she escaped, but when she was thirteen, a man from Kaleva was shipwrecked on the North Farm beach and Louhi was at last hopeful of getting her Sampo.

The witch woman recognized the castaway immediately as Väinämöinen, the spellsinger whose magic powers were said to rival her own. "He's not only famous for the charms he can work, but he's also rich," she said to her daughters. "And it's well known he has no wife." She gave a final pat to Lahja's hair while Kaisa and Toini made rude faces behind their hands.

"He's the worst one yet," Toini said gleefully when Louhi had gone to conduct their guest from the sauna. "Did you see him? He's *old!*"

Lahja had indeed seen the wrinkled, gray-bearded, sea-soaked, shivering man her mother had led from the beach to the bathhouse. Surely not him! she thought, clasping her arms against a chill of her own.

"He must be at least a hundred," Kaisa said as she poked Lahja. "Imagine having to go to bed with him!"

Lahja didn't want to imagine it, not any more than she had wanted to imagine a wedding night with any of the suitors. Her father had said not to worry, that he would see that she wasn't forced into anything against her will, but who was he to go against the will of Louhi?

The sisters continued to tease, and Lahja bit her lip and forced back tears. Louhi would be angry if she appeared red-eyed before the guest, so she contented herself with glaring at her tormentors.

"What an ugly face!" Toini shook her head reprovingly. "What if Mother should see it? Or worse yet, your gray-bearded lover. Aren't you supposed to look *beautiful* for him?" She did a cross-eyed, limp-wristed imitation of a simpering maiden.

As Lahja exploded with rage, a hate-charm of her mother's sprang into her head. "Move quickly like a swift hound," she hissed, pointing her finger. "Blaze like a spark; turn their eyes around, make their heads shake, their bones rattle, their breath come short."

A roar filled Lahja's ears as the air in the room seemed to take shape and move. Kaisa and Toini cowered against the stove bench, clutching their heads and chests, and Lahja stood frozen. After a timeless moment, when she could breathe again, Lahja fisted her hand and blinked to clear her mind. *What had she unleashed?*

There was no time for recriminations, questions or apologies. The door opened and Louhi stepped over the sill, followed by the old man, Väinämöinen, and then by Taisto. The three girls, only partially recovered from their fright, took positions behind the already spread table.

"You'll eat with us," Louhi said to the guest. "There is no enmity between us now. I can offer only dry bread and a bit of salmon, I'm sorry to say. Not even a mouthful of beer. It's a bad time in Pohjola, but you're welcome to share what we have." She led him to the best seat and filled his plate.

"I'm grateful," Väinämöinen said. For an old man, his voice was surprisingly strong. He looked across the table at the girls.

"My three daughters," Louhi said as they each curtsied.

Väinämöinen, as always happened at such introductions, gazed the longest at Lahja. "I've heard of that one," he said. "She is known by report even in Kaleva."

Louhi did not quite hide a smirk of satisfaction.

"She is very dear to us," Lahja's father said.

Louhi nodded. "Yes, very dear. There is only one thing that would ever induce us to part with her."

Väinämöinen raised his eyebrows, but he did not ask the expected question. He ate heartily of the plain fare, conversing about farm matters with Taisto and smiling impartially at all three girls. To Lahja he looked like a kindly grandfather. She couldn't imagine him in the role of a suitor, nor did he act the part. When the meal was finished and Louhi suggested that Lahja show their guest about the farm, the girl felt none of her usual reluctance.

"Get him to demonstrate some of his magic," Louhi whispered as she took Lahja aside. "And pay close attention to the results. I need to know just how adept he is. If he hasn't the skill. . . . "

Louhi did not finish the sentence, but Lahja could guess what she was thinking. If Väinämöinen could not make the Sampo, there would be no point in entertaining him further. Her own thoughts leaped forward. The calf would have escaped once more. Perhaps . . . it would be so easy. . . .

"And no lying about it," Louhi said with an eagle's penetrating gaze. "You can be sure I'll know. Now go. He's waiting, and I'll be waiting as well."

Lahja wrapped herself in a woolen cloak, for winter was once more keeping a late grip on the northland. As they walked, Väinämöinen admired the sturdy log farm buildings and the well-repaired fences, clucked sympathetically over the still frozen, barren fields and the few thin cattle, and kept a respectable distance from his guide. "You needn't be afraid of me," he said as they leaned on a fence rail. "I know what your mother expects, and I can't say that the thought of such a beautiful young wife is disagreeable to me. But I courted a maiden once who was unwilling, and it ended badly. I won't repeat my mistake. So even if I can pass your mother's test, it's still up to you." He smiled wryly, smoothing his beard. "I know my age and my appearance are against me, but my farm is a prosperous one, and my wife would never want for comforts." He described his rich fields and plump cattle, his full storehouses and his manor house that was always warmed with fires and cheerful with good company. He didn't voice the implied comparison to desolate North Farm. He didn't need to.

Quiet Water Farm. Lahja savored the name, imagining it as a place of dappled sunshine on still ponds, of smiles and pleasant voices never raised in anger.

But to go with it all . . . an aged husband. Lahja tightened her fingers on the rail. Was it always going to be such a choice?

"So." Väinämöinen blew a breath of steam. "I have to pass your test as well as your mother's."

Lahja said nothing. Surely he didn't expect an answer so soon.

"You must take your time," he said. "I'll wait. But in the meantime, can you tell me what it is I have to prove to Louhi?"

"That you can truly work magic," Lahja replied. "Mother needs you to make something for her. She'll explain what it is. But . . . perhaps . . . can you show me a bit of what you can do? Just a sample, some simple thing."

He smiled. "You name it."

They walked again, this time along the rock-strewn beach. Lahja tried to think what would impress her mother, and pointed to a stone. "Can you make bark grow there?" It was a trick she had seen Louhi do when *she* wanted to impress a stranger.

Väinämöinen's mouth moved, but Lahja could not hear the words of his chant. She stared at the stone, and as she watched, a layer of bark grew and covered the entire surface.

"Touch it," Väinämöinen said. "See if it's real."

Lahja did, and it felt exactly like the bark of a tree. Louhi's magic bark always melted away when someone touched it, but this remained solid under Lahja's hand. She peeled off a finger's length to show her mother, and even then it stayed intact.

"Anything else?" Väinämöinen looked smug.

Did he know that he had shown up Louhi? Feeling an unexpected surge of familial loyalty, Lahja disliked his expression. They passed a large chunk of washed-up iceberg, clear and blue in its frozen purity. "Can you break a fence rail from that ice?" Lahja asked, knowing that not even he could accomplish so large a transformation.

He did it easily, and again the magic-formed rail felt solidly real. "Come here," he said, leading her to a cove where the remains of a boat lay scattered on the rocks. "I built that myself, with help from woodworking spells. Unfortunately, it couldn't withstand your northern seas. Though now that I'm here, and I've seen you"—she definitely didn't like his expression then as he regarded her—"I'm thinking that those spells worked in my favor

34

better than I thought when I was floundering in the icy waves."

So he could even spell himself a boat. Lahja's heart sank. Surely, such a spellsinger could create Louhi's magic mill. She glanced at the old man quickly, then away before he could see the trembling of her lips.

He saw, and shook his head sadly. "What can I do to make you like me better?"

He *was* kind, Lahja thought. Maybe. . . . She looked down at the bark fragment still in her hand, and curiosity overcame her reluctance to accept anything from him. "How did you do this?" she asked. "Would you tell me the charm you used?"

His drooping eyelids lifted in surprise. "Why would a tender blossom like you want to know that kind of wizardry? I should think . . . living with Louhi . . . you must know such knowledge is full of dangers."

Lahja nodded. She knew it very well, but still—"I'm just curious, that's all. I already know some charms, like the one for getting the butter to come and the beer to ferment. I've used them—before the famine, that is, when we still had cream to spare, and barley and hops." Everyone knew those charms, but Lahja didn't tell Väinämöinen that for her they seemed to work exceptionally well, nor did she tell him about the revenge charm that had so frightened her and sisters earlier that day.

Väinämöinen continued to regard her bemusedly. "Does your mother know of your interest in spellsinging?" he asked.

"No," Lahja said hastily. "And please don't tell her. She wouldn't like it at all."

"No, I expect she wouldn't," Väinämöinen agreed. "People like us are jealous of our secrets and our powers."

Lahja felt rebuked. "Then—forgive me for asking," she said.

"Please, don't be annoyed." Väinämöinen raised a conspiratorial finger. "I'll tell you what. If it works out between us—if I please your mother, and if you agree to come away with me—I'll gladly teach you all you want to know." He drew closer and peered into her eyes. "I suspect you may have some talent for these things. As the daughter of such a powerful spellsinger, it wouldn't be at all surprising."

A spellsinger. It was a far better term than "witch," the appellation that was usually applied to Louhi. Lahja had never wanted to be like her mother, and before now hadn't even wanted to imagine what her special efficacy with household charms might signify.

"Think about it," Väinämöinen said. "As a husband, I would deny you nothing."

If only he hadn't said the dreaded word. Not all the kindness in the world could make up for what it implied, or for the decrepitude of his person. As they returned to the farmhouse, Lahja wrapped her cloak tightly about her against a coldness that had nothing to do with the weather.

Louhi met them at the barnyard gate. "Well?" she said, pulling Lahja aside with no regard for civility. "What did you find out?"

Lahja showed the bark and described the fence rail. She didn't mention the boat until her mother, aware that she was holding something back, forced it out of her.

"A boat! He charmed himself a boat!" Louhi shouted. She cackled in triumph as she embraced Väinämöinen.

"Remember—it sank," he reminded her as he extricated himself.

"Never mind that. You're the one—I knew it from the first." She pulled him by the arm. "Come along, let me show you what I want." She led him out the gate and over a frozen field, to the mountain cave where she had labored so unsuccessfully to forge her Sampo.

Lahja followed slowly, kicking with her boots at the icy clumps of earth. If Väinämöinen could make the Sampo, according to her mother the fields would be green again. No babies would cry from hunger, and even the poorest house would be warm in winter. Of course she wanted it to happen— it would be inhuman not to—but why did she have to be the bribe?

Lahja waited near the mouth of the cave, and the others were not long inside. Louhi came out with the face of a storm cloud, and Väinämöinen looked crestfallen, too. "I'm sorry," he kept repeating. "I would do it if I could. Truly. For the maiden." He caught sight of Lahja, who stood just within earshot, and made a *moue* of disappointment.

"Oh, I believe you," Louhi said crossly. "Why would you refuse, if you had the ability?" She gave a bark of scorn. "Hah! You're not as powerful as I've heard."

Väinämöinen replied meekly. "Perhaps not. I can charm wood easily; metal—no. For that you need a blacksmith with some skill at spellsinging."

Louhi regarded him intently. "Do you know of such a person?"

"It so happens I do."

"Can you send him to me?"

Väinämöinen appeared to reflect. "If you'll get me safely home. I seem to be stranded here, without a boat or sleigh or money. And even if I had the means, I'm not sure I could find my way back."

This time Louhi considered. "I'll provide you with a horse and sleigh. And a driver. He can return with your blacksmith."

Väinämöinen extended his hand, and they sealed the bargain.

Lahja trailed after them as they returned to the house. It was a reprieve, but for how long? A blacksmith, she thought. Someone huge and hairy and covered with soot. Even Väinämöinen seemed better by comparison. She dragged her feet crossing the field, and in the barn, where her father rationed mouldy hay to a single thin-flanked cow, she threw herself tearfully into the arms in which she had always found comfort.

"There, there." Her father wiped her eyes with a corner of his barn smock. "This is all for nothing. Väinämöinen is leaving—they stopped by and told me. So you're safe. You're safe with me."

If only it were true. "Only until the next time," she said with a hiccup. "The next one—he could be even worse."

Taisto sat her down on the milking stool. "Lahja. My gift. My precious one. Listen to me. Whoever he is, you needn't marry if you don't wish it. You have my promise. Don't you believe me?"

"But the Sampo—"

He looked quickly around the empty barn, then forced a tight smile. "We'll get along. We have, up to now."

Lahja remembered when the stalls had been crowded with heavy-uddered cows, when forkfulls of sweet hay had streamed from the loft. Her father's cheeks had been full and rosy, not gaunt and pale as they appeared now.

If it was in her power to restore all that. . . . "I do believe you," she said. "But. . . . " She couldn't finish; couldn't force him to insist again that their poverty didn't matter. She kissed him and returned to the house, where her mother and sisters were laying out another meager meal.

Väinämöinen, who was to leave in the morning, stayed for supper and spent the night on one of the benches. Neither he nor Louhi nor Taisto had much more to say, and the evening was an awkward one. The night, to Lahja, was worse, with Väinämöinen snoring and her own troubled thoughts keeping her awake. Some time well after everyone else was asleep, she felt Toini rise from their pallet bed, heard her fumble in the darkness for her shoes and cloak, then slip quietly out the door.

No one else stirred. Lahja thought at first her sister was going to visit the outhouse. But no—Toini hated the cold and would have used the night jar. Lahja suspected then that she was going to meet someone. Probably a certain darkly handsome reindeer herder. She had come upon Toini talking to him just the other day in their camp beyond the far pasture.

"Don't tell Mother," Toini had begged, and Lahja had acquiesced. Now, she had a new anxiety to ruin her sleep. Whatever plans Louhi had for her two older daughters, Lahja was sure they didn't include wandering Lapp herdsmen.

What if Toini had run off? Louhi would be furious. Lahja fell asleep worrying about her own complicity, and in the morning she was vastly relieved to see Toini safely back in bed.

The reindeer herders left that day for a new camp, and Toini was crosser than ever. Väinämöinen left, too, in a borrowed sleigh, with repeated promises to send it back with the blacksmith.

"His name is Ilmarinen," the old spellsinger shouted over his shoulder as the sleigh moved through the gate. "He doesn't talk much, but he can make music with hot metal. Treat him well and you won't be sorry!"

Lahja was already sorry. The huge, hamfisted iron-pounder she had pictured was now in her imagination a grunting mute as well. Kaisa and Toini whispered together and smirked, and she was sure they had much the same thoughts.

*   *   *

> "You yourself, smith Ilmarinen, . . .
> If you hammer out the Sampo
> And devise its ciphered cover,
> You may have the maid as payment,
> Have the lovely for your labor."
>
> The Kalevala, Runo 10

Ilmarinen came with the spring rains. He left the mud-mired sleigh at the pasture gate and slogged his way to the house, where Lahja and her sisters viewed his dripping figure with alarm.

"Get off our clean floor!" Toini screeched, pushing him back to the doormat of green boughs. Kaisa ran to get their mother from the pantry, and Lahja tried to hide behind the table.

He was the blacksmith of her worst forebodings: huge and somewhat stooped, with shoulders and arms that looked ready to burst from his clinging, wet coat. He grinned foolishly as he greeted Louhi, twisting his cap in his hands as he tried to back out the door.

"I'm sorry . . . such a mess . . . shouldn't have come in."

"Of course you should," Louhi said, glaring at Toini. "Just take off your coat and boots." She motioned to the girls to help him, and Lahja gingerly pulled at one sleeve. As it slid off, it revealed an iron-hard forearm corded with muscles and the hamlike, soot-ingrained hand she had expected.

"You must be Ilmarinen," Louhi said, and he agreed with a duck of his head.

"My friend Väinämöinen said you had need of my services."

At least he could talk, Lahja thought. And his face wasn't really so bad. He had a strong nose and jaw, white teeth that were a bit crooked, and ears that stuck out from his close-cropped hair and beard. All in all, not quite an ogre.

"Yes, I have a job for you," Louhi said as she led him to the table. "But first, something to eat. And would you like a sauna? From the looks of you, you've had a hard, wet journey."

"Yes, thank you, I am hungry. But the sauna I'll take after I finish my work." He fell to his bread and salt fish and cold porridge with a good appetite, and while he ate, Louhi whispered to Lahja to put on the silk dress.

She did, hiding behind the mosquito curtain, clenching her teeth against the ignominy of once more being put on display.

Louhi came to inspect, fastened a necklace of colored stones around Lahja's neck and pinched her cheeks. "Smile!" she commanded. "This is the one. I know it—I have the feeling."

Louhi had had the feeling before, but Lahja didn't remind her. This time she, too, felt her fate descending on her.

Ilmarinen stared, speechless, as Louhi led her youngest daughter from behind the curtain. "And did Väinämöinen tell you about the reward, if you're successful?" she asked.

The blacksmith gulped and nodded.

Louhi stretched her face in a thin-lipped grin of triumph. "Then I suppose you'll want to get to work right away."

Ilmarinen glanced through the window, at the rain still pouring down in gray sheets. "I prefer to work outside, and I can't set up my forge in that."

"It's already set up, inside a cave," Louhi said. "That's the way *I* prefer it, away from prying eyes. Can you manage that?"

Ilmarinen looked again at Lahja, gulped once more and agreed. "I'll get my tools from the sleigh."

"I'll go with you," Luohi said. "And show you to the cave."

They left, braving the rain. Lahja thought her mother might have waited, at least until the storm abated. Given the poor man a chance to dry out. Why did the woman have to be so eager? Lahja sighed as she took off the silk dress, and Kaisa surprised her by helping to fold it and lay it back in the chest.

"It's so lovely." Kaisa stroked the soft material. "Perhaps now Toini and I will get to wear it."

"You!" Toini hooted. "You'd burst the seams."

Lahja winced for Kaisa, though it was true that the middle sister stayed round-figured even on famine food. Kaisa's lower lip trembled, and Lahja patted her arm. "I'm sure it can be altered," she said. She herself would be glad to see the last of it, if only it didn't mean the end of her maidenhood. "You're lucky," she said to both sisters. "To stay here with Father. Not to be . . . bartered. Why should you *want* to wear the dress?"

"What do you know about it?" Toini turned on her with a face distorted by venom. "What do you know about being left out, being passed over, not even being considered? What do you know about spending the rest of your life serving *her*?" She pointed in the direction of the cave.

Lahja didn't know what to say. Toini was only seventeen, and she had always been so proudly superior. "You mean . . . you would have considered marrying any of the ones who came?"

Kaisa answered. "In a minute."

Toini lifted her chin. "Speak for yourself, Sister. As for me, I'll only settle for someone a lot better looking than any of the yokels who've been panting around our little royal beauty. But as long as *she's* here"—the bitterness in her voice intensified—"what chance do either of us have?"

Lahja looked to Kaisa for confirmation.

"Yes," she said, "for our sakes, please take the blacksmith."

"She'll have no choice," Toini said with smug finality.

Lahja didn't tell them about their father's promise. They probably wouldn't have believed it. She didn't know that she did either, entirely, but she clung to it as to a lifeline.

Louhi spent the afternoon with Ilmarinen in the cave. The girls occupied themselves with weaving, but all three pairs of eyes strayed more often to the window that faced the cave than fastened on their shuttles. Lahja, especially, made a mess of her fabric. How could she concentrate, knowing now how avidly her sisters hoped for Ilmarinen's success? She felt more trapped than ever.

When Louhi came in, Toini jumped up first. "Can he do it?" she asked as she helped her mother off with her wet cloak and headscarf.

"He's going to try," Louhi answered. She looked tired, too tired to even scold about the mistakes on the looms.

"Where is Father?" Lahja asked, badly needing his support and reassurance.

"He's gone to the fishing grounds," Louhi said. "Pray he's successful, now that we have such a hungry mouth to feed." She frowned at the remains of the loaf that Ilmarinen had so quickly demolished.

Lahja clasped her hands. Yes, she would pray that he returned soon.

"How long will the blacksmith be here?" asked Kaisa, who had begrudged him every bite of the loaf.

"As long as it takes," Louhi replied. "He won't be a bother to us, except for the food. He wants to sleep in the cave—to keep his fire hot, he says—and even to take his meals there."

Lahja suspected it might be shyness that induced the big man to want his privacy, and she liked him better for it.

Louhi gathered together another scant meal—this time with only half a bread loaf—and tied it into a cloth bundle. She handed it to Lahja. "Here—

you can take this to him now, for his supper." She quirked up one side of her mouth in a lopsided smile. "And to encourage him."

Lahja wrapped herself in a sealskin and hurried out. The rain still hammered down, and the field she crossed was a morass of mud. She kept the food dry beneath her cloak, but her boots were thick with mire and her skirt hem sodden by the time she reached the cave.

Smoke billowed out, but inside, under a high, vaulted ceiling, the air was breathably clear. The blacksmith stood bent over his red-hot forge, and Lahja approached the fire gratefully.

"Blacksmith!" she called, and he turned to her a soot-smeared face.

"What are you . . . this is no place for you." He wiped his hands on his leather apron. "I told your mother—"

"That you wanted to be alone. I know, and I won't stay. I just brought your supper." Lahja handed him the bundle.

He appeared so embarrassed, shifting his feet and looking everywhere but at her, that she started to back out hurriedly.

"Wait! I didn't mean . . . at least, stay and get warm." He dragged a boulder near enough to the fire for warmth but safe from flying sparks.

She returned and sat primly, toasting her booted toes. Ilmarinen sat on another stone and quickly dispatched his meal. "I'm sorry there isn't more," Lahja said. "For three years now, we've been on famine rations."

He nodded sympathetically. "Such a hardship. Especially for someone so young." He stared at the delicate hands she held clasped around her knees. "But you . . . look well."

"No—yes—I mean, I haven't suffered." She leaped up, hoping he hadn't noticed her flush. Hoping he would never know why she had escaped the hunger and hollow cheeks of other Pohjolanders.

"I'm glad," he said. "Someone like you should always be well cared for." He stood, too, and peered into the molten metal at the bottom of his forge. "And if the Sampo works—you always will be."

Lahja puzzled over his words. Did he mean, because she would be with him, or because Pohjola would be prosperous again? Perhaps, like Väinämöinen, he would grant her the right of refusal. She was afraid to ask, and said nothing. She tried to look into the forge, too, but the heat seared her face. She wondered how he could stand it.

"Not so close," he said, leading her back to the rock. His hands were blacker than ever and thickly callused, but she didn't find them offensive. She thought, why should I be repulsed by the signs of honest work?

She pointed to the forge. "What is in there? What is it you're melting?"

"Precious things," he answered. "Your mother gave me gold and silver, all of it pure. Her entire hoard." He indicated Luohi's treasure cask half hidden under a projecting shelf of rock. "A magical device like the Sampo can only be made of the finest metals." He moved to the forge again and pumped the bellows. The fire burned hotter, casting a red glow over his angular features. "It's time to test it," he said. "If you don't mind . . . I need to be alone now, to concentrate."

Lahja got up hastily. She guessed there were spells involved, and that they they must be done in secret. She started to wish him luck, but when she thought of everything involved if he should be successful she contented herself with a brief "good night" and hurried out.

Smoke was still issuing from the cave when Lahja and her sisters went to bed, and in the morning it was coming out thicker than ever. Had the smith slept at all? Lahja wondered. She braved a sleety deluge as she took him his morning's porridge, and as she neared the cave metallic fumes mingled with the wood smoke and the icy rain to form a vaporous blanket that obscured the opening.

Lahja blundered her way through it and into the arms of Ilmarinen, who was on his way out.

"Oh! I . . . so sorry . . . I was just going to. . . . " He gestured vaguely at the field outside, then turned red through the soot that begrimed his face. Without meeting her eyes, he bolted.

Lahja blushed for him, too, then giggled. What if she had come a minute later and caught him releasing his stream? The poor man would probably have taken off back to Kaleva, on foot and without a word.

When he returned, Ilmarinen went directly to his forge. He pretended to be too busy to speak to her, or even to look at her, so Lahja waited.

Finally, after too long a silence, she asked how the work was coming.

"Not so well," he said with a grunt. He reached with his tongs to pick up a lump of half-melted gold. "I thought I had the outer shell formed, but it cracked and now I have to begin all over again." He shook his head and frowned. "It's difficult. More difficult than I thought."

Lahja unwrapped the porridge bowl. "Then you must rest, and eat." Probably, she thought, he had hammered all night.

"What will it look like, when it's finished?" she asked while he ate. The Sampo she had seen in her vision had been too luminous for her to discern its exact shape or features.

Ilmarinen drew with a stick on the cave floor. Released from his embarrassment, he spoke easily, even eagerly. "The outer shell is round, and about this size." His circle had a diameter of two and a half or three feet. "The metal must be pounded thin, yet it has to be strong. My first attempt had a weakness, here." He indicated a spot on one side. "Inside, it will have three compartments. Three individual grinding mills, each with its own pouring spout. Three strong legs—here and here and here—to anchor it to the ground, and the lid"—he reached for a square of white birch bark on which various ciphers were inscribed—"it's the most important of all. I have to duplicate these ciphers exactly, so the lid will turn and the three grindstones move."

Lahja examined the strange marks. "What do they mean?"

The smith shrugged. "I don't know. They're probably powerful magic. Too powerful for the likes of me. I only know simple spells, like one for making the fire burn hotter and one for shaping and one for cooling. Your mother"—he glanced warily at Lahja—"she says I'm to forget these as soon as I finish inscribing them. She says she'll spell me to make sure I do."

"This one looks familiar." Lahja traced the most prominent figure. Something icy touched her spine, and she dropped the bark.

"It's best not to look too closely," Ilmarinen said.

Lahja believed it. The Sampo was to be no ordinary mill. She hoped its magic wouldn't mark its maker; the blacksmith didn't deserve to be harmed because he knew too much about Louhi's witchcraft.

"I'll leave you to your work," Lahja said. She would have liked to stay, to watch him at the anvil, but he did not issue an invitation. He went back to the forge, and she slipped out of the cave.

Ilmarinen's second attempt at the Sampo went back to the fire, too, as did his third. His face and arms became blacker and the furrow between his eyes deeper with each day's failure, but he refused to admit defeat. Lahja continued to bring him his meals, and as their conversations became more relaxed, she looked forward increasingly to the visits. He told her about his childhood, his fascination from boyhood with working metals, his father's recent death. He described his farm, Ilma, which his mother and sister were tending while he was gone. She told him something of her own life, but only about the comparatively happy times before the famine had brought hunger to her countrymen and jealousy and scheming to her family.

Louhi visited the cave often, too, and returned each time with her lips more tightly drawn. Lahja and Kaisa and Toini kept out of her way, and so did their father when he returned empty-handed from his fishing. "I'll give him one more day," Louhi muttered after Ilmarinen had been with them for a week and she had measured the diminishing flour in her bin. She handed Lahja the blacksmith's dinner bundle. "Tell him. One more day. I can't feed him any longer than that."

Lahja slogged through the muddy field. It was the coldest, wettest spring she could remember. The sky was forever dark and gray, and the rain never stopped. The farmers couldn't plow or plant, and there was no new growth anywhere, not even in the forest.

It was a dead world, Lahja thought. For some reason, Ukko frowned on the northland. Perhaps the god was working against Louhi and Ilmarinen. Perhaps he was even angry with them and wished them harm. Perhaps, even now. . . .

There was no smoke coming from the cave. Lahja ran the last few yards, her mouth dry and her heart pounding.

Inside, at first she feared the worst. The fire in the forge was out, and Ilmarinen lay slumped half over the anvil.

Dead, she thought, but as she approached she saw that he was only sleeping. And beside him, on the floor, stood the completed Sampo: round and fat-bellied, with three mouths and a lid that shimmered with all the colors of a rainbow. The inscribed ciphers danced before Lahja's eyes, but otherwise the mill was quiet and unmoving. Beautiful, but not yet alive.

Ilmarinen stirred, rubbed his eyes and looked up at Lahja. "It's finished," he said, the pride in his voice overcoming his sleepiness. "Go and tell your mother."

Lahja ran back across the field, then crossed it once more behind Louhi. At the cave, Louhi told her to wait outside, but curiosity drove her to crouch at the entrance where she could see what was happening within.

Ilmarinen joined her, also shoo'd out by Louhi. They watched while the witch woman muttered incantations over the Sampo and set its lid to spinning. Louhi stepped back, and the mill appeared to grow in size and brightness until Lahja could barely stand to look at it.

A grinding sound came from within the Sampo's belly, soft at first and then louder, until the entire mill began to vibrate. Louhi raised her arms and chanted again, and the mill's three legs appeared to fasten themselves to the floor of the cave.

"I've got to see this better," Ilmarinen said. He crept closer, and Lahja followed. Louhi, absorbed in watching the mill, took no notice of them. The grinding continued, with the mill now steady except for its spinning lid. After a few minutes, something issued from each of the mouths.

Louhi uttered a ringing laugh. She held her opened hands beneath the first spout, and they quickly filled with kernels of grain. The second spout poured out a steady stream of what looked like salt, and from the third came a rain of gold and silver coins.

Ilmarinen held his hands beneath the salt spout, and Lahja captured in hers a mound of coins. She laughed aloud, too, until she withdrew her hand and the coins melted away.

Louhi's grain and Ilmarinen's salt disappeared as well from their hands. The Sampo kept grinding out more, but it all vanished as soon as it hit the floor.

Another of her mother's illusions! Lahja could have cried with disappointment, but Louhi did not appear dismayed. "Yes! Yes!" she crowed, blowing kisses to the Sampo. "My beauty! My treasure!" As she danced around the shining mill, she finally registered Lahja's and Ilmarinen's presence. "What are you two doing here?" she demanded with a fierce scowl. "I told you both to stay out. Now go! Outside the cave. Now!" She flapped her hands at them, and they ran. A rumbling followed them, and moments later Louhi herself exited the cave. The rumbling grew louder as rocks fell from above, stirring up a great cloud of dust. When it settled, huge boulders and a mound of rubble completely blocked the entrance to the cave.

Ilmarinen looked stricken, and Lahja shared his anguish. After all that work! Louhi alone appeared unfazed. She put an ear to the largest boulder, made the sign of triumph and motioned for Lahja and the blacksmith to listen, too.

At first Lahja heard nothing but a faint hum that could have come from within her own unsettled head. But then it became clearer, and she recognized the sound. It was the Sampo, still grinding away within the cave.

"And look!" Louhi cried, pointing up at the sky.

Lahja realized that the rain had stopped. The sun shone bravely through a few wisps of cloud, and in minutes they too melted away. A rainbow spanned the blue vault, the wet brown earth steamed gently, and the very air felt fresh and warm and rich with promise.

Louhi grinned hugely. "It's beginning already. Now—just wait see. All those doubters—they'll see who is truly the greatest spellsinger."

Her mother had certainly out-magicked Väinämöinen, Lahja granted. Whatever the Sampo was doing inside the mountain, its effects continued outside as the bright sun drove away the last vestiges of winter. Lahja and Luohi removed their cloaks as they walked back to the house, and Ilmarinen raised his bare, black arms to the warming orb. "I'll take that sauna now," he said. "Then"—his teeth gleamed whitely as a smile split his sooty face—"then we'll talk about my reward."

Lahja cringed. She had hoped, after all their talks, that he had come to look upon her as something more than his prize. That her wishes might be important, too. She had hoped . . . but Lahja suddenly did not know the huge figure who loped ahead of her, shouting for water and towels as he raced toward the smoking sauna. In the cave, he had been gentle and subdued. And always considerate. This leaping, shouting wild man . . . no, he wasn't the same person at all.

She had to find her father, quickly. Louhi ordered her to the sauna, to prepare it, but she was already on her way to the barn. Let Toini or Kaisa see to Ilmarinen's bathing; she had more important matters—her very future—

to safeguard.

"A promise is a promise," her father said, after she had tearfully explained. "But perhaps—there may be a way. This blacksmith—is he so repulsive to you?"

Lahja answered truthfully. "No, I rather liked him, at first. Until he made the Sampo and now expects me to go away with him. I . . . I can't. I'm not ready for . . . all of that." She wrung her hands as she pleaded. "Please, if you love me, don't make me go!"

Louhi came into the barn, wearing her angry face. "What is this all about? Girl, stop that sniveling and go to the house. And you"—she addressed her husband—"how can you listen to her?"

Lahja could hear the sound of their heated argument as she lingered outside the barn, but she could distinguish few of the words. Louhi's voice was the loudest, but her father's the most persistent. She crossed her fingers and repeated a charm to ensure wishes as she picked her way across the barnyard. Already the mud was drying, and a bird sang from its perch on a fence rail. If the Sampo magic continued, there would be calves bawling again in the large pen, pigs rooting in the small one, chickens scratching in the kitchen garden— and it was unthinkable that she not be here to see it.

At the house, Toini and Kaisa were arguing over the silk dress. "Oh, take it," Kaisa finally said. "Mother says we'll soon be able to buy others. She's promised me a new one for Midsummer Eve."

"Or for the wedding feast," Toini said, turning to Lahja. "When is it to be?"

"Nothing is settled," Lahja said.

Both sisters eyed her apprehensively. "You haven't . . . you wouldn't . . . you *are* going to accept him, aren't you?" Kaisa asked.

"He would be a powerful enemy," Toini warned.

"Please, I can't talk about it." Lahja sat down at the table and buried her head in her arms. If only her decision were to affect only herself. She had heard the word, "war," in her parents' argument. She knew what refusing the blacksmith would mean to her sisters, and that was bad enough, but was it possible that she would also be responsible for renewing the enmity between the two countries?

After a long hour, Ilmarinen came in from the sauna. Well-scrubbed and flushed from the heat, dressed in clean clothing, Lahja barely recognized him. The steam appeared to have removed his earlier bravado as well as his layer of soot. He seated himself a distance from Lahja, at the foot of the table, and studied his fingernails.

He finally looked up at Lahja. "Where are your mother and father?" he asked. "We have much to discuss."

46

"Dowries and such," Kaisa said with a giggle.

"They'll be here," Lahja said just as they came in, Louhi first and Taisto trailing behind. A bad sign, Lahja thought, but her father gave her a ghost of a smile and she relaxed slightly.

Ilmarinen stood and approached the couple. "Are you satisfied that I've performed my part of the bargain?"

"There's no doubt of that," Louhi said.

"Then you'll accept me as a son-in-law?"

Taisto cleared his throat.

"Is there a problem?" the blacksmith asked.

"Only when it comes to time," Louhi said. "The girl is yours, if you care to wait. At present, she is too young to be a wife."

"Thirteen, I believe," Ilmarinen said. "Others that age have married."

"This one is not yet a woman. If you know what I mean." Louhi looked archly at Ilmarinen, whose sauna-flushed face grew even redder.

Lahja blushed, too, and stared at the floor. Her mother knew very well that Lahja had packed moss between her legs three times already, but she wasn't about to reveal the lie. If it bought her more time. . . .

There was a long, awkward silence.

"You do understand?" Lahja's father said. "We always meant, some years in the future."

"Years!" Ilmarinen's jaw dropped. "How many?"

"We'll let you know," Louhi said. "We'll send for you when the time is right."

Ilmarinen sighed. "Is this your wish?" he said to Lahja.

"Yes," she whispered, unable to meet his eyes.

"Then, it's settled." Louhi shook Ilmarinen's hand. "Toini, Kaisa, bring food," she ordered. "We'll have a betrothal supper. Simple, I'm afraid. But the feast will come later."

"No, don't bother," Ilmarinen said. "I'll start back right away, if I can borrow a horse or a boat. I've already been away from my farm too long. I'll get my things together. . . . " He backed himself out of the door.

Louhi didn't conceal her relief. "Take one of the boats," she shouted after him. She assembled a food pack and handed it to Lahja. "See him off. Be polite, but not too encouraging. He is, after all, a foreigner."

Lahja found Ilmarinen on the beach, loading the smaller of the two fishing boats. She could find nothing to say, and neither, it seemed, could he. She finally mumbled an "I'm sorry," but it wasn't until he was ready to cast off that the blacksmith found his tongue.

"I'll fix up the house," he said. "I'll build another room, with a proper bed, like the one your mother has. I'll build a new stove with a chimney, so you won't have to wash soot from the walls. I'll make everything nice for you. Just—don't have me wait too long."

He was gone, and Lahja didn't know whether she was relieved or sorry.

* * *

> The new Sampo then was grinding,
> With its ciphered cover spinning;
> Ground three binfuls every morning:
> First a bin of things to eat,
> Next a bin of things to sell,
> Last a bin of things for home.
>
> *The Kalevala*, Runo 10

In Pohjola, it was the most glorious spring in memory. Streams ran sparkling and clear, the grass in the meadows had never been more lush, grains sprouted and throve as if by magic, and in every wooded glade the bushes bent heavy with berries. Kaisa finally got enough to eat, and she grew round as a barrel. Toini revelled in her fine dresses and their father in his new herd of cows. Louhi employed a house maid and a milk maid, and the master a host of field workers. The house boasted a new table inlaid with golden figures, and the barn received a new roof. There even seemed to be fewer mosquitoes than usual.

Lahja rejoiced in the prosperity and in her freedom from any more suitors. She spent happy hours roaming the fields of North Farm, feasting on wild strawberries and stretched out in meadows watching the birds and dreaming that she was one of them. Whenever she thought of Ilmarinen it was with guilt, but not enough to make her send for him. Her father was content to keep her at home, and Louhi, now that she had her Sampo, appeared to have put the blacksmith out of her mind.

A year went by, and no one at North Farm mentioned the maker of the Sampo. Lahja began to wonder why he did not come, himself, to remind them of the promise. Was it possible that his affections had not been truly engaged? Or perhaps some southern girl had captured his fancy, one who didn't send him away with false excuses. She didn't like the idea at all.

A second year passed, and again the summer seemed longer and the winter less bitter than before the Sampo. Lahja, though she told herself that everything was perfect, grew unaccountably disturbed whenever anything— even Toini's new ornaments or the mention of metal-working—reminded her of Ilmarinen. What if he were still waiting for her to send word? She had appreciated his shyness before, but . . . surely there was such a thing as being too diffident.

Though Lahja's ambiguous position still kept the suitors at bay, a speculative look began to return to her mother's eyes. Louhi started urging the family beauty to go with her sisters to the northland gatherings, to the sleigh races and bonfires and harvest festivals, and Lahja feared that avarice had once more entered her mother's heart.

In the third year, Kaisa became betrothed to an upright lad from a neighboring farm. Toini continued to be choosy, claiming that she couldn't abide the wind-chapped fishermen or the farmers with manure on their boots. Lahja had other suspicions, however, and they were confirmed when the reindeer herders returned, including the handsome, dark-eyed one, and her sister again sneaked out at night.

A famous warrior, one Lemminkäinen, came from Kaleva to court Lahja, but Louhi had heard he was already married and sent him on his way. "There'll be others," the witch woman said confidently. When Lahja hesitantly reminded her of Ilmarinen, she only laughed. "He's given up on you, and it's to our advantage. A poor blacksmith—we can do much better than that."

So it was starting again! Lahja wanted to protest, to insist that she be left in peace, but the habit of obedience was too strong. She would have liked to send a message to Ilmarinen, but after all the time that had passed she was too proud. Whenever she looked toward the Sampo mountain she thought of him, and it became more and more difficult for her to even be polite to the new crop of suitors.

Fortunately, none of them pleased Louhi. "He must be someone wealthy," she insisted. "Someone who can command a host of warriors." For North Farm in its new prosperity was once more the target of marauding raiders. Louhi's treasure cask was almost full again, and she stated repeatedly that she would only accept a son-in-law who could add to it and protect it.

By late fall the third year of the Sampo, no one had qualified. There had been no new visitors for several weeks. Soon the north would be winterbound. Lahja was beginning to breathe easier when on a November day the watch dogs' howls warned the household of the approach of strangers. Taisto hurried to the high back pasture to see who was coming, and reported both a boat with red sails approaching on the bay and a basket sleigh along the shore.

He couldn't tell from the distance, and through the light snowfall, if they were raiders or friendly callers. Louhi cast a rowan branch into the hearth fire to divine the answer. She sent a maid to fetch her battle armor if the sap from the branch should ooze out bloody, and another for a jug of welcoming mead if it should run clear.

Lahja and her sisters watched nervously, but the sap was neither red nor white. The burning wood began to drip with honey, and Louhi uttered a triumphant cry. "The best sign of all—mighty suitors are coming!" She sent the maids to spy on the approaching visitors, to determine whether they traveled light or bore rich gifts.

The boat, the servants reported back, was heavily laden, but the sleigh, though elaborately decorated and festooned with bells, appeared to contain only the rider.

Lahja had a premonition, a sense of something or someone familiar, and ran into the farmyard to see for herself. She climbed a fence and squinted to focus through the drifting snowflakes. In a moment of clarity she knew both visitors. The bearded man standing at the stern of the boat, steering it through the incoming tide, was surely the old spellsinger, Väinämöinen. The man in the sleigh, resplendent in a fur coat and a high, peaked cap, was none other than Ilmarinen.

He had come at last! Lahja raced back to the house with her news.

Louhi reacted as Lahja might have expected. "Two suitors, is it?" She pursed her mouth. "Not a hard choice, I'd say." She fixed Lahja with her gaze. "Not when one comes with gifts, and the other empty-handed. When one is a high-born man from a wealthy estate and the other is a lowly blacksmith. When one is a famous spellsinger of proven reputation and the other a would-be wizard with a mouthful of empty lies."

What lies? Lahja started to ask, but she refrained from defending Ilmarinen. Let her mother think she would be guided; that she was still biddable.

Louhi handed Lahja the two-eared pitcher of mead which, according to custom, a maiden was to offer to her chosen suitor. "There must be treasures in the red boat," the greedy witch-mother crooned. "Golden combs and jeweled belts and shoes of the finest leather. Snow white linens and soft rugs and plates of hammered silver.

"And the blacksmith"—she made a disparaging noise and spat—"he no doubt expects you to be thrilled to launder his blackened clothes and wipe the sooty sweat from his brow. Not very appealing, is it?"

Lahja remained silent. Louhi patted her arm, checked that the pitcher was full, and went to the window.

Väinämöinen arrived first, his face blue and his beard stiff with rime, but with his eyes gleaming. "I heard that you were not yet married," he said to Lahja at the doorstep. "I thought, why not try again? My boat is loaded with gifts for you and your family. Am I welcome?"

Lahja greeted him courteously and invited him in, but she did not offer him the pitcher. She ignored Louhi's frantic motions, left Toini and

Kaisa to help the spellsinger out of his snow-covered outer garments, and waited in the doorway for Ilmarinen.

He came running from his parked sleigh. "Am I too late?" he gasped. "I tried, but the boat was so much faster. Has he . . . have you . . . ?"

"No, you're not too late," Lahja said. When she offered him the pitcher, Louhi groaned and threw up her hands. Lahja hoped the blacksmith didn't notice.

He did. "My future mother-in-law isn't pleased," he whispered after he had drunk.

"She'll get over it," Lahja said. She prayed it was true. In any case, Ilmarinen was here, dressed as a proper suitor in all new clothes, and there was the old promise that Louhi could not ignore.

Taisto offered the blacksmith a warm welcome, but Louhi continued to be grudging. "There are still tests," she said during supper when Ilmarinen asked about the wedding date. "Nothing is settled yet."

"But . . . I made the Sampo, and Lahja is now willing." The puzzled young man looked from Lahja's father to her mother.

Taisto raised his eyebrows and shrugged. Väinämöinen, who had accepted Louhi's invitation to stay the night, smiled, and Lahja turned angrily to her mother. "What do you mean?"

Louhi flicked a pointed tongue across her lips. "That three years have passed, and how do I know he is still worthy?"

"I haven't changed," Ilmarinen said.

"Then prove to me that you can protect our daughter. I won't send her away with a weakling."

The blacksmith flexed his right arm until the muscles rippled, but Louhi only sniffed. "That's nothing." She leaned toward him. "I understand you have a farm. In the morning I'd like to see you plow. I have a field that's never been turned. A nest of poisonous vipers lives there, and none of our workers will touch it. Can you do this for me?"

Ilmarinen paled, but he nodded. "I'll do it."

"Mother!" Lahja started to protest, but Louhi showed her a stony face, and she knew it was useless.

It was useless, too, to appeal to her father, and that night before they all retired she sought out Väinämöinen.

They whispered in the fireplace corner. "You told me once you would teach me charms," Lahja said.

"That was when I thought I might win you," he replied. "It seems now you have made your choice."

"I have, but"—she took his hand—"Ilmarinen is your friend, isn't he? Do you want to see him bitten tomorrow by a viper? He could die!" Lahja allowed a tear to glisten on her cheek.

Väinämöinen patted the soft hand. "Don't cry, child. Yes, I believe I can help you. I was going to tell you the charms anyway, as a wedding present, but I may as well begin now." He put his mouth to her ear. "Listen closely— this is one to ward off snakes."

Lahja repeated the charm after him. Ilmarinen came jealously to the corner to see what the whispering was about, and Väinämöinen left the lovers to their few moments of private conversation before Louhi intervened.

It was enough time, however, to teach him the charm. In the morning, Lahja watched from the fence while Ilmarinen began to plow. His strength was more than equal to the difficult task, and three straight furrows glistened before the first viper raised its hissing head. Then, each new clod of upturned turf lifted more angry serpents to the surface. Lahja added her voice to the plowman's to calm them before they could strike.

"Foul creature, get out of the way," she chanted, concentrating all the force of her will. "Who raised your head up? If indeed you lift it up again, Ukko will crush you with hailstones."

The serpents slid back meekly into the ground, and neither Ilmarinen nor his horse was harmed. By mid-day the field was plowed.

When Louhi came to inspect, she did not appear pleased. "That's only the first test," she said.

Lahja clenched her fists within her gloves. She knew the stubborn set of her mother's jaw, but she also knew a hardness growing within herself. In this instance, she vowed, Louhi would not have her way.

With Lahja's help, Väinämöinen's bear and wolf charms worked on the next trial Louhi set for him. Ilmarinen presented the witch with two fresh skins, but she still demanded a final proving: a giant pike, to be caught without net or spear, in the freezing waters of the bay.

Lahja went once more to Väinämöinen, and again he obliged. This time, however, Ilmarinen had to do his spellsinging alone. Lahja paced the shore while the blacksmith tried vainly to sing the monstrous fish into his boat. She called out the charm, too, but she was too far away for her words to be effective. If only she could be there with him. . . . But Louhi, guessing that Lahja was somehow aiding her lover, had forbidden it.

The fish began to swim away. The charm was not going to work, Lahja realized. Ilmarinen rowed after the scaly creature, which was almost as large as his boat, but it submerged and was lost to sight.

A lone eagle circled overhead. Lahja remembered her mother's transformation, that she had witnessed as a child, and she remembered too the words that had produced it. Without thinking, she raised her arms and shouted them into the wind.

The wind lifted her, and she was airborne, soaring and circling, look-ing out through eyes not her own. She swooped with powerful wings, and with iron-hard talons fastened on the flash of silver that was the pike and carried it to shore.

"Lahja! Are you all right?"

It was Ilmarinen, bending over her. She was stretched out on the beach, her arms and legs weak and a roaring in her ears.

When the noise subsided and she could sit up, Lahja saw that Ilmarinen had landed the pike. "The eagle did it," he said. "Then it flew away. Incredible luck."

"Yes," she agreed. She started to ask him if he had seen her disap-pear from the beach, but decided she really didn't want to know.

Together they dragged the pike to the house. Louhi finally had to admit herself satisfied, and with winter's breath blowing colder every day, set a near date for the wedding.

* * *

There was salmon on the platters
And beside it pork aplenty;
Cups were brimming, bowls all heaping
For the pleasure of the feasters,
Most of all the son-in-law.
The Kalevala, Runo 21

Louhi, once she accepted her defeat, spared no expense for the wed-ding feast. The house at North Farm was scrubbed and shining: the walls whitened, the floorboards smooth as silk and the ceiling covered with silvery bream scales. The tables groaned with food, and the guests who crowded the benches were scrubbed and shining, too: the men in their brightest winter-lined jackets, with their beards neatly braided, the women displaying their costliest ornaments.

After the feasting, and after Väinämöinen had entertained the crowd with his singing and harp playing, it was time for the serious business of the day—the instruction of the bride and groom.

Lahja, on the women's side of the room, peered through her veil at Ilmarinen where he sat in the highest seat on the men's side. His face was flushed from too much drink, and she wished they could leave while he could still walk to the sleigh.

She wished they could leave, too, before Louhi forgot her company manners and began to rail against her missing eldest daughter. Toini had cleverly taken advantage of the occasion to disappear during the night with the reindeer herders, knowing full well that her mother would be too busy to organize a pursuit. Louhi had had to be satisfied with muttered imprecations and with "why's?" and "how could she's?" which she repeated at intervals even during the feasting.

Lahja knew why she had done it. For the last two months, in the sauna, the increasing roundness of Toini's belly had told her. She and Kaisa had promised Toini not to tell, but Kaisa had whispered during Väinämöinen's singing that now she was no longer bound. Lahja wanted to be well away when the explosion came.

But first she had to endure the tedious instructions which the bride must receive within hearing of all the guests. Lahja had heard them before, at other wedding feasts, and thought them quaintly humorous. She wondered why everyone around her looked so serious.

As the favored daughter of North Farm Lahja had had few responsibilities, and the stern-faced old crone who took on the role of instructor reminded her that all that was due to change. "Going to another household as a wife and daughter-in-law, everything will be different," she warned with a shake of her head. "There will be no more lolling about in the fields watching the clouds."

Now how did she know about that? Lahja wondered. No, she didn't like this part of the ceremony at all.

The tutor continued. "At home, your parents have been lenient. Going to your husband's home, you must learn to watch your step. To conduct yourself with caution." She enumerated the wife's daily tasks: getting up before dawn to light the fire, feed the cattle and muck out the barn. Then, back in the house, she must wash the baby, scrub the floors and tables, carry wood, grind grain, count the spoons, tote water, heat the sauna, all the while bowing down humbly and speaking gently to her in-laws. Above all, she must never gossip, and never allow herself to stretch out lazily on the stove-bench or flop down even for a minute on the bedding.

The old woman shook a bony finger at Lahja, and other voices added to the list of wifely chores. There would be butter to churn, bread to bake, beer to brew and dishes and clothes to wash. There would be spinning and weaving and entertaining the neighbors, all to be done with unfailing good humor.

Lahja took it all as well as she could, her eyes fixed meekly on her clasped hands. Once she sneaked a glance at Ilmarinen, but he was grinning foolishly at the back-slapping men around him and she couldn't tell whether he shared her dismay. She knew many of these women; knew their bad tempers and the short shrifts they took with their housekeeping. Now, catechizing the neophyte, they had all become paragons of virtue. Perhaps Toini had chosen the right course, Lahja thought; there would be no floorscrubbing in a Lapp tent.

Ilmarinen, when his turn came to be instructed, had it much easier. He had only to drive his sled carefully on the wedding journey so as not to tip his bride out on the snow, to see that she didn't have to bake famine bread, and if it was necessary to switch her, to do it where it wouldn't show.

At the last instruction, the women stood up as one and hooted. Väinämöinen plucked a loud chord on his harp, but the cat-calls and laughing commotion went on. Louhi took advantage of it to duck out the door, after whispering to Lahja that she had something for her—a farewell present—from the storehouse.

The storehouse. The noise around Lahja faded as an icy foreboding gripped her. Toini wouldn't have fled empty-handed. If Louhi were to open her treasure cask, what would she find?

Lahja forced herself to move, out the door after her mother. She was halfway up the storehouse path when she heard Louhi's piercing scream.

"Fiends! Thieves!" More shrieks issued from the hut. "Ungrateful spawn, may she rot in Tuonela!"

Lahja ran the remaining distance. Inside the storeroom, her mother stood over the opened casket. When she saw Lahja, she broke into fresh outcries. "Half of it gone! Gold and silver and jewels. The strand of pearls that was to be yours!" She slammed down the casket lid, revealing the broken lock, and her face assumed its fierce eagle expression. "How dare she!" Her fingers formed claws. "I'll hunt them down. I'll tear him apart. I'll—"

Lahja formed eagle thoughts of her own as she faced her mother squarely. "You'll leave them alone," she hissed as the iron-hard power built in her.

Louhi backed off, staring. "You! How did you . . . when. . . . "

"I learned from you," Lahja said.

Louhi continued to stare, but she relaxed her claw hands. Lahja eased herself, too. "Toini and her man will be long gone," she said in her normal voice. "It's unlikely you'll find them among the reindeer people. It's unlikely you'll find them at all."

"Some day I will," Louhi said.

Lahja thought, it was a meeting she would be happy to miss. Louhi turned her attention to the casket lock, muttering a metal-working charm, and Lahja slipped from the room.

She found Ilmarinen outside, harnessing his horse to the decorated sleigh. He looked a bit unsteady on his feet, but she expected that the cold air would sober him up quickly enough. If not, she could take over the driving.

She had never done it before, but as the old crone had told her, and as she herself now knew with a certainty, there would be many changes in her future.

Four

Lahja the Wife

ဆ ✿ ಐ

Untamoinen . . . took this Kullervo
Took the son of Kalervo
And sold him to smith Ilmarinen,
Cunning craftsman of the hammer.

The Kalevala, Runo 31

So what am I supposed to do with this fellow?" Lahja's hands-on-hips posture reflected her irritation. Ilmarinen had just presented her with his new slave, and like the majority of his well-meaning gestures this one had the potential of being more trouble to her than benefit.

She didn't like the looks of the young man. He was sturdy enough— some might even call him handsome, with his yellow hair and ruddy complexion—but she had been disturbed by the flash of wildness she had seen in his eyes before he lowered them meekly. She perceived, too, an insolence in the way he held himself, even with his head bowed and his cap clasped in his two hands.

For someone so young, he had already achieved an unenviable reputation. Lahja scowled as she took her husband aside. "I've heard the talk about this Kullervo. You must have, too. Doesn't know his own strength, and ruins everything he attempts. Untamoinen couldn't train him to do anything useful, so how do you expect me to do any better?"

"You have your ways," Ilmarinen said.

He was referring, she knew, to her spellsinging, which was always a sore point between them. It gave a woman too much power, the men of Kaleva thought. Ilmarinen approved of it only when it worked to his advantage, as in the charms Lahja sang to protect their cattle, the milk charms she chanted in the barn and the corn-growing charms in the fields. Though he hated the nesessity, he had come to depend on the results. In the four years Lahja and Ilmarinen had been married, the blacksmith had spent more time at his forge than on the farm. That Ilma had sustained them in the hard times, which had fallen on Kaleva was mostly due to Lahja's efforts, and they both knew it.

Her marriage hadn't turned out as she had expected, though Lahja couldn't have said now what had been in her sixteen-year-old mind. Certainly not the numbing before-dawn chores in the barn, the hours behind a plow or the tedious grinding in the grain shed. And especially not the two dead babies; the tiny graves on their lonely, wind-swept hill. Lahja's slender figure had thickened at the waist and her hands had coarsened. Her spun-silk hair, no longer as glossy, was now decently covered by a matronly kerchief, and her feet no longer skipped when she walked.

Ilmarinen was a good enough husband—better than most, Lahja supposed. There had been no beatings, few quarrels and even moments of surprising transport. But while the direst predictions of the old woman at the wedding feast had not come to pass, the sour-faced crone had been accurate in her warning that there would be no leisure to lie in strawberry fields and dream of flying.

Ilmarinen glanced from his frowning wife to the slouching youth. He shook his head and frowned, too. "I thought you'd be glad. I bought him for you—to help out when I'm busy smithing. It's not proper that you should be out in the fields. If people saw you, what would they say? This fellow can relieve you of all that." His voice took on an aggrieved tone. "I thought I might at least hear a word of thanks."

Lahja did not soften. "How much did you pay?" For all their joint efforts, their savings in skins and coins did not cover the bottom of a chest. She had been hoping for a horse and sleigh of her own when the pile grew higher.

"I got him cheap." Ilmarinen's pout eased into a grin. "A couple of old pots, some used hooks and sickles and hoes. I think Untamoinen was glad to get rid of him."

Lahja sighed, partly in relief and partly in exasperation. At least Ilmarinen hadn't impoverished them, but—if she had wanted a servant, it certainly wouldn't have been this one. On Untamoinen's farm, she had heard, he had built a fence without a gate, ruined a threshing and rendered a field barren with his curses. And Ilmarinen expected her to make use of him.

"I'll be working at the forge all week," the blacksmith said. "I've got that iron bench to make for Antero, then a bunch of ornaments for his wife. I thought this boy could do the plowing."

"We'll see," Lahja said. She thought: I'm not about to let him ruin *my* fields. But she would find something useful for him to do—there was certainly enough work on the place. She admitted to herself that her husband had meant well, and finally gave him the thanks he expected.

Ilmarinen, satisfied, returned to his smithy under the oaks for some evening labor, and Lahja showed the slave, Kullervo, to the barn where he would sleep. "There's plenty of straw; you'll be comfortable enough," she said.

"Yes'm," the youth acknowledged with a nod. He was younger even than she had thought at first, Lahja observed as she studied him more closely. His downy cheeks showed no trace of a beard, and his wide, full-lipped face had an unformed, childish cast. Lahja usually felt drawn to young creatures—colts and lambs and most of all, children—but there was something about this lad that she sensed was not right.

He continued to hold his cap between knob-knuckled hands that looked disproportionately large even for his brawny frame. His jacket, Lahja noticed, was threadbare and his trousers had no padding.

It was still cold at night. "I'll get you a blanket from the house," she said.

He started to follow her, but she motioned him back. "You wait here. There's nothing for you to do right now—I've finished the milking. So take it easy. Get acquainted with the cows. I'll bring you your supper."

"Yes'm," he said again. Did she detect a shade of disappointment in his face? Surely he wouldn't expect to eat with them—not a bought slave. So maybe, as the gossip went, he had once belonged to a noble family, but that was long ago, the family slaughtered and he still alive only because a few farmers were willing to put up with his surly antics. Cursing a field! Threshing rye to a pulp! He'd better not try any of that with *her*.

Lahja carried a blanket and a bowl of stew to the barn before she called her husband to his supper. Kullervo received them gratefully, with a shy smile that momentarily lightened his sullen features. He had probably known little kindness in his life, Lahja guessed. Small wonder that he had grown up warped. Her sudden surge of sympathy caused her to linger, to question him about his farming skills.

Did he like animals? she asked.

He did, but Untamoinen hadn't trusted him with his cows.

Did he know carpentry? There was a shed that needed repair.

He did, but after the fence debacle he hadn't been allowed cutting or hammering tools.

The slave spoke well, and he didn't appear stupid. Lahja inspected him again, keenly. "What about that fence? Eight feet high, and no way to get in or out. What were you thinking of?"

Kullervo stared at his knuckles. "He said I was a bastard, and that my father deserved what he got. He was my uncle, you know. Untamoinen was. And he raised me as a slave."

Maybe it was true—Lahja didn't know. Kullervo had been born to a servant girl, one of Untamoinen's brother's household, all of whom it was said

Untamoinen had massacred.

Kullervo looked up, and dangerous red flames shone deep in his eyes. "I meant to show him that he can't escape me. That some day. . . . " His voice dropped away, but the knuckles cracked with a loud report.

Lahja suppressed a shudder—she wouldn't want him for an enemy. She took the empty bowl. "Will you work for me, without mischief?" she asked.

He returned her gaze through slanted eyes. "You are very beautiful. Though some people say you are a witch. Is it true?"

She straightened indignantly. "That's none of your affair. I asked you: will you work for me?"

"If you treat me fairly," he said. "This is my time of waiting, and it has nothing to do with you."

Waiting for what? she wanted to ask, but didn't. She had no desire to be involved in feuds, and even though Untamoinen was their neighbor, she owed him no obligatory warning.

Besides, he would probably laugh. Kullervo looked harmless enough now, spreading out his straw and settling himself for sleep. "Do you want me to help with the morning milking?" he asked.

Had Untamoinen believed he would bewitch the milk? Better to be cautious, Lahja decided. "No, the cows are used to me," she said.

He smiled. He knew it was more than that, Lahja suspected. He knew she was more than a bit afraid of him.

It would have to change. In the morning she would establish her authority firmly, she told herself as she left the barn. She could treat the fellow fairly, yet brook no spellsinger's tricks. He had the power—she had seen it in his flaming eyes. Untamoinen had done well to be wary.

Thank you, Ilmarinen, she thought bitterly. A fine present her husband had given her. She called to him from the barnyard gate, that his supper was ready, then hurried to the house to get it on the table before he came in.

The blacksmith ate quickly and noisily, without words. He had washed at the smithy, as was his custom, but as usual he hadn't done a thorough job. His face was still soot-streaked and his hands made smudges on his bowl, but Lahja was so accustomed to his appearance that she made no comment. She would gladly have heated the sauna for him nightly, but he insisted that a once a week scrubbing was enough.

No, nothing had been as she had expected. She had wanted flowers on the table and conversation and a clean husband, but she had given up the first when she found she couldn't have the others. Then she had wanted babies, but . . . though the tiny graves weren't Ilmarinen's fault, she had felt her heart harden against him.

He was good at his work. Everyone said so, though Lahja would have preferred pay in coins rather than praise or promises. But no one in Kaleva had wealth to spend, for while Pohjola in the north continued to prosper, the southern regions suffered a succession of droughts and floods and too-hard winters. Lahja had begged Ilmarinen to make another Sampo, for them, but try as he might the smith could not remember the runes he had inscribed on the magical cover of Louhi's mill.

"Is there more stew?" Ilmarinen asked, and Lahja replenished his bowl. At least they had food enough, though the promised extra room and the bed off the floor had failed to materialize. Lahja thought often, wistfully, of the comforts of North Farm. Ilma was poor by comparison, and no amount of magic charms could make it otherwise.

Lahja washed the dishes while Ilmarinen sat by the fire. "How did you get on with the new fellow?" he asked.

"I don't trust him," she replied. "There's something . . . damaged about him. And I'm almost sure he can work spells."

Ilmarinen snorted. "Not likely—who would have taught him? Anyway, you can handle that sort of thing. Didn't your mother teach you counter-spells along with everything else?"

His face took on the hardness it wore whenever he spoke of the witch of the north. Louhi was hated more than ever in Kaleva, the beleaguered farmers blaming her and her magic mill for every cattle plague or crop failure. Ilmarinen now cursed the day he had made the Sampo, and Lahja didn't dare to remind him that he had done it for her.

How quickly love could change, she thought. Four years ago Ilmarinen hadn't minded that she was Louhi's daughter. Now, it was a bitterness that he could not leave alone. She had never told him that it was Väinämöinen who had taught her the charms she used on the farm. He would have reacted jealously, and the old spellsinger was one of their few friends.

Lahja ignored the mention of her mother. "Can't you use a helper at the forge?" she asked. "Now that you have this big order. . . . "

"You know I only work alone," he said.

Except that time in Louhi's cave, she thought. You didn't mind my company then. Now, they stayed apart during the day, and in the increasingly rare occasions when their bodies joined on the straw pallet it seemed to Lahja they were strangers coming together.

"Is there some reason *you* don't want him around?" Ilmarinen eyed her suspiciously. "Just how were you planning to spend your day? Were you expecting company, perhaps?"

"Of course not!" These new suspicions were a recent development, another burden. Antero, when he had come to commission the bench, had looked at her for a few seconds too long and Ilmarinen had accused her of flirting. And Toini's husband, the one time the couple had visited, had aroused in him the same unfounded jealousy.

Lahja couldn't understand it. She saw herself as spent and faded, no longer anyone men would look on with desire. Yet, she remembered, the slave Kullervo had thought otherwise. *You are very beautiful*, he had said.

Lahja shuddered. What if Ilmarinen had heard? What if he said it again, when Ilmarinen was around? What if he looked at her a minute too long? Her head began to ache and she finished her work quickly, scrubbing the table with the last of the water in the pan.

She would send the slave to work well away from her, she decided as she lay beside her snoring husband. He could go with the cows, and neither she nor Ilmarinen would need to see him all day.

When Lahja finally fell asleep she dreamed of her father, who had been dead for a year. He seemed to be warning her of something, but she couldn't understand his words. If only she could have attended his burial, she thought for the hundredth time. Then, she might have been able to communicate with his spirit. But Ilmarinen had forbidden her to make the trip, saying that with the enmity between the two countries it was too dangerous to travel.

It wasn't the real reason, Lahja knew. The blacksmith had been afraid she wouldn't return.

He needn't have worried. "You should have trusted me," Lahja whispered to his sleeping back. "I wouldn't have deserted you." Without her father, there would have been nothing to keep her at North Farm. No, this was the life she had chosen, and she would make the best of it.

Lahja rose before dawn, as always. She started a fire, mixed the day's bread dough and set it to rise, then headed for the barn.

She found Kullervo already half finished with the milking. "I told you I'd do that," she snapped. Couldn't he follow simple instructions?

The slave smiled ingenuously up at her. "You see, they give me their milk gladly."

Indeed, Nervy, the most stubborn of the cows, was releasing frothing streams into the pail. "What milk charms did you use?" Lahja asked.

He continued to look innocent. "I don't know what you mean."

"I think you do." When he didn't answer, she shrugged. If he had charmed the cows, he was doing them no harm. In fact, quite the opposite. "I'll leave you to it, then," she said. "Afterwards, you can take them to pasture. I'll bring you a lunch along with your porridge." There was no need for him to come to the house, and after breakfast Ilmarinen would be gone.

"So I'm to be a cowherd?" His smile assumed a wry twist.

She wondered what he had expected. "You'll find it easy enough," she said. "Find them a grassy meadow, and watch out for bears in the woods."

"I think I can manage that," he said. "But I had hoped. . . . "

He didn't finish, but the open admiration in his gaze revealed his thoughts plainly enough. Lahja felt herself color, and hurried away before he could notice. Such impudence, for a slave! She would have to set him straight, and no mistake, before a dangerous situation developed.

She tended to the pigs and the new calves, then, back at the house, she kneaded and shaped the bread loaves. She set aside the one for Kullervo's lunch—she had an idea how to tell him, without words, that she was no one to be trifled with.

Outside, she quickly found a smooth, hard stone the size of her fist. She shaped the loaf around it and put it to bake with the others. She knew a moment's misgiving when she imagined the slave breaking a tooth, but reassured herself that it was unlikely. However, he would get a surprise, and if he had any wits at all, a warning.

Ilmarinen came in from firing up his forge, already covered with a layer of soot. Lahja set his breakfast porridge before him, along with a chunk of yesterday's bread.

"I'd rather have that," he said, sniffing at the baking loaves.

Lahja poked one, but it was far from done. "You'll have to wait, then."

But please don't, she prayed as through the window she saw Kullervo approaching from the barn. The slave was certainly a fast worker, she granted, but hadn't she told him plainly not to come to the house?

Ilmarinen rose from the table. "No, I'd better get to work," he said, and Lahja breathed a sigh of relief. She watched as the two men met outside, but they exchanged only a few words before they parted.

Lahja brought the slave's porridge to the door. "I told you to wait at the barn," she said.

"I'm not allowed to even see the inside of your house?" His gaze was plainly, inexcusably, mocking.

"Not unless you're invited." She shut the door in his face.

Afterwards, she was ashamed of her rudeness. But it was for his own good, she rationalized. He had to learn his place.

He would, when he broke open the bread.

Pleased with her plan, she smeared butter on the warm, stone-filled loaf, added a chunk of cheese and wrapped it up in a cloth bundle. She found Kullervo waiting at the barnyard gate, the cows in a docile line behind him.

He accepted the food with thanks, but managed to touch her hand when he received it. Lahja glared and retreated behind the fence.

"I might watch over your cattle better if you sent me off with a smile," he said.

"Just do your job," she replied crossly, waving him off. Then, a fear crossed her mind. Would he dare harm her cows?

"Wait!" she called, and climbed the fence to shout a protective charm after the retreating animals. "Go my cows, to the grove, to the open clearings," she chanted. "Watch over them, Maid of the Forest; keep them from harm's way."

Kullervo looked back and grinned at her. Go ahead and laugh, she thought. Maybe tonight you won't feel so cocky.

She watched until the cows and the herder disappeared into a copse of alders. Smoke issued from the smithy hill, and she could imagine Ilmarinen hard at work. If he looked down he would see her lazying against the fence, and the possibility was enough to make her move away quickly. Ilmarinen hated idleness; she only wished he loved farm work as much as he did pounding iron.

After her morning chores in the house and barn, Lahja set out for the south field to finish the plowing. Let Ilmarinen worry about what the neighbors might think. They seldom had visitors, and if he were really so concerned he could have done it himself days ago.

Lahja inspected the sky and nodded in satisfaction. If the good weather held—she crossed her fingers—she could get the field harrowed and planted in the next few days. Oats, she decided; they were the least risky in these bad luck times, and their grain supply was almost depleted.

At North Farm, she couldn't help thinking, since the time of the Sampo they had eaten soft wheat bread. And Louhi's daughters had never harnessed themselves to horses and plows.

But that was then, and this was now. Grasping the plow handles with calloused hands, Lahja trudged over the clods of upturned earth, furrow after crooked furrow, until her back and arms were a continuous fiery ache. At the end of a particularly hard patch she sat on a stump to rest and to wipe the sweat from her eyes.

It seemed to her at the moment that her last four years had been spent in harness. That instead of escaping by marriage from Louhi's domination, she had found a harsher servitude. And one that offered no promise of change.

A line of gulls flew overhead, heading in the direction of the sea. A single eagle glided even higher, circling over the forest. Lahja followed the winged creatures as they dipped and rose, envying them their freedom. Once, she recalled, she had soared with them in her imagination, but now she was too earth-bound for such fancies. She lowered her gaze back to the field, estimated the harvest that would see them through another winter, and with a sigh returned to her plow.

By the end of the afternoon she regretted the suspicions that had led her to assign the new servant such an easy task. He should be the one stumbling across the field, aching with weariness. Tomorrow it would be different, she vowed. He would be chastened, and she could sit on the stump all day and direct him.

He was late returning with the herd. The mosquitoes were especially bad, and Lahja had already lit smudge fires in the barn field where she would do the milking when she heard the herdsman's horn.

The cows looked sleek and well fed, their full udders swinging heavily, but there was something oddly skittish in the way they acted. Even Apple, Lahja's favorite, shied away when she approached.

Had Kullervo bewitched them, after all? Lahja recited a calming charm as she stroked Apple's flank, and the cow finally quieted. Kullervo watched with an expressionless face that reawakened Lahja's distrust. "I'll milk them myself tonight," she said.

"As you wish." He turned away, but not before she detected a faint smile that she couldn't interpret. She wished he would say something about the stone in the bread. She wanted to ask, but didn't dare.

He answered her unspoken question by holding up a broken knife. "It was my father's. The only memento I have of him." He sounded coldly angry, and flames burned deep in his eyes. "It's ruined now, thanks to you and your trickery."

Lahja bit her lip. It wasn't the result she had expected, but she didn't know how to undo the harm. "I'm sorry," she said. "Perhaps Ilmarinen can repair it."

"It wouldn't be the same." He shoved the knife back into his pocket and strode stiffly to the barn.

Lahja followed, to fetch her stool and bucket from the milk room. She ignored Kullervo, who stood staring into a corner, and returned to the cows.

She placed her stool beside Apple, and again the cow seemed not to recognize her. She repeated the gentling charm, and after that, one she often used while milking. "May rivers of milk flow," she chanted as she squeezed the teats. "May rapids of milk foam into my pail."

Apple shifted her feet, lowing softly, then switched Lahja with her tail.

"Don't do that!" Lahja scolded. She jerked the tail sharply, and Apple's lowing became a growl that should have come from a forest beast. The cow's smooth hide was suddenly transformed, before Lahja's eyes, to a shaggy pelt, and the rank odor of bear invaded Lahja's nostrils.

She screamed as sharp teeth bit into her leg and a bear's claws raked her chest. She fell backwards into a black pit of pain, and when she opened her eyes she saw Kullervo's triumphant face looking down on her. His laugh mingled with her shrieks as the bear tore at her again, and beneath the pain she felt her life ebbing away.

There was nothing she could do. Whatever spell Kullervo had worked, she was too weak to counter it. Ilmarinen, if he heard her screams, could not come in time. The farm dog cowered by the fence, and the eagle circling overhead was indifferent to her plight.

The eagle. . . . Once, she remembered, she had entered an eagle's body. The words came back to her, and with the last of her strength she whispered them from the bottom of the pit.

Gliding low on a current of air, she looked down with detachment on the broken, lifeless body in the field. She could never enter it again, but the regrets she felt were lost in a flood of new sensations. Another existence was opening to her, and she spread her wings and soared.

Five

Louhi

ဢ ✿ ର

"Do not now, dear mother-in-law,
Ask me that about your daughter,
Where she lives or how she prospers."

The Kalevala, Runo 38

OUHI KNEW AS SOON AS SHE SAW Ilmarinen's sleigh coming out of the woods that he carried bad news. She had dreamed the night before of death, and in the morning the sun had risen into a blood red sky.

As he drew closer, the smith's appearance did nothing to allay her fears. She sharpened her vision to focus on his haggard face and bloodshot eyes. His clothing looked as if he had slept in it for at least a week, and as he climbed out of the sleigh and walked slowly toward the house, his whole person appeared diminished in size.

She did not come out to meet him. Ilmarinen had not once brought Lahja to visit, not even for the funeral rites of her father. It would have been difficult, she granted, with their two countries warring, but for Taisto's sake she couldn't forgive him for not trying.

Taisto had been so bereft when Lahja left. . . . It was no secret that he had loved her the best of their children. Better even than herself, she admitted with a bitterness that tightened her lips as she waited in the doorway.

The blacksmith stopped before her and bowed his head. "Don't ask me," he begged. "Don't make me tell you."

She took pity on him. "Just look at me," she said.

She read in his eyes her daughter's terrible end, and her cry split the clouds and bent the trees in the forest. In the farmyard it sent every animal scurrying for cover and every servant into hiding in fear for his life.

She didn't repeat it, but stood arrow straight and stone faced, silent except for the cracking knuckles of her tightly folded hands.

"I c-could do nothing," Ilmarinen stammered. "N-not even revenge myself on that demon Kullervo." He fisted his own hands. "I've hired men to comb the province, but he's vanished as completely as the Hiisi-spirit that must have bred him."

"You can leave the revenge to me." Louhi pinioned the white-faced blacksmith with her accusing gaze. *Yes, squirm, you lily-livered, spineless excuse for a husband.* He could have protected Lahja if he hadn't been so enamoured of his ironwork. If he hadn't bought the cheapest slave available, to free himself for his forge.

"It wasn't my fault," Ilmarinen continued to plead. "You know how I valued her. You, more than anyone, know how I labored to win her." He looked toward the rocky hill where the Sampo lay buried. "How I worked for your benefit even against my own country."

He was contemptible, Louhi thought. Not worth her anger. "I didn't mean, revenge against you," she said, releasing him from his fear. "This Kullervo—tell me about him." She motioned him into the house.

She listened intently while Ilmarinen related all he knew about the slave and about his wife's death. "He must have enchanted the bear," he concluded. "Or else he enchanted Lahja, to think the bear was a cow. She was lying over the milking stool, with the pail near her hand."

"Powerful magic," Louhi muttered. But she could counter it. She would have to if she were to set herself against him. She directed Kaisa, who was living at the farm since her own husband's recent death, to lay out food for Ilmarinen, and while he ate she stared fixedly into the fire.

"Arise, my Nature," she murmured softly. "Come, O Nature of my ancestors. Clothe me and lift me up that I may see that which is hidden."

The pine log had been burning all day. Its red glow seared Louhi's eyes, and when she closed them she sank easily into the desired trance. After long years of practice, she no longer needed the external aids of other shamans—the fasting, the furious drumming and the hour-long chants—to accomplish her goal. By sheer willpower and a few properly chosen words she could slip into the other world, and by directing her inner vision she could, in most instances, find what she sought beyond the temporal veil.

This time Louhi saw the still youthful Kullervo in his death throes, and she heaved a satisfied sigh. She would need to do nothing—the yellow-haired one carried within himself the seeds of his destruction.

The room swam as she came back into her body. "Fetch me water," she commanded Kaisa. When she had drunk and bathed her eyes, she threw the rest on the fire to propitiate and settle the spirits. Then she turned to her son-in-law, to share with him her reassuring vision.

Ilmarinen sat stuffing himself, bread in one hand and meat in the other, grease running down his chin. He had never been noted for his delicate manners, Louhi recalled, but this . . . she glared at him in disgust.

The blacksmith ignored her look of censure. "I haven't eaten so well in years," he said. "No one in Kaleva has." He eyed the well-laden table. "I see the Sampo is still working for you."

Louhi did not deign to answer. Nor would she tell him about her vision, she decided. If his grief could be cured so easily with a haunch of pork, he didn't deserve to know Kullervo's fate.

Ilmarinen continued to eat, all the while staring at Kaisa with the same greediness with which he devoured the food. Kaisa, plumper than ever and rosy from the fire, grew even redder under the smith's scrutiny.

"Don't look too hard," Louhi warned. "Lahja's sister is already promised." She narrowed her eyes. "For the second time. Her first man was killed by one of your people, in a battle over a single sack of grain."

Ilmarinen, if he heard, took no notice. "You still have the Sampo," he said. "And I have no wife. It would seem that you owe me."

Louhi fixed on him a look of pure venom. "I owe you nothing," she said. "It would be best if you left now. You've delivered your evil news, so be on your way. If any of my countrymen find you here, I can't answer for what they might do."

Ilmarinen did not move. "I can remember when you were more hospitable. But that was when you wanted something from me." He glanced outside. "It will be dark soon. Can't I at least spend the night?"

Louhi shrugged. She folded her arms and turned her back on him. "You can sleep in the barn, but be gone by morning."

She didn't move until she heard the door close behind him. Then, weary beyond words, she sank down upon the hearth bench.

Yes, she had been rude, but who could blame her? Owe him? When she had given him her dearest treasure?

Taisto hadn't been the only one who had loved Lahja. Admitting it after all the guarded years, Louhi felt something twist within her. Such feelings, never allowed expression, had become a deeply buried canker.

Love? Even now she scarcely dared think the word. And she had certainly never said it, not even to her husband. For the feared Witch of the North there could be no trace of human weakness; nothing that might diminish her in the estimation of both subjects and enemies.

"We are not like others. We can't afford to be," her shaman father had told her when it was apparent that she, and not one of her brothers, was to inherit his mantle. "And as a woman, you must be doubly careful. You must be invulnerable."

She saw in her mind a tiny, black-haired girl who had not really understood all that her father was saying. She only knew how proud she was to be singled out for the teaching, how relieved that her terrifying voices and visions and embarrassing "fits" were no longer to cause her ridicule.

"Your mother should have told me sooner," her father had said. "I've been looking for signs in the boys, but I never suspected that you—" He had embraced her, for the first and last time. She could still feel the roughness of his beard and smell his smoky, bitter-herb scent.

After that there had been only stern words and endless charms to memorize, punishing fasts and dizzying sessions with the drum. But there had been rewards, too, when she had left her body and circled the treetops, when she had kindled fires with a touch and turned drops of water to ice.

"You are the hope of Pohjola," her father had told her repeatedly. Other wizards could imitate perfectly the screech of an eagle while pretending to ascend to the sky, and more often than not the spectators believed the performance to be real, but Louhi had the rare, true gift.

Her father's fellow wizards all acknowledged it. "She will lead our warriors in battle," they said. "At last we can win back land and fill our storehouses with plunder. At last the Kalevalanders will quail before us."

The prospect of power was heady to a twelve-year-old girl. And when her father took her to see the poorer regions of Pohjola, the barren fields and the starving children, she was filled with a holy zeal. Ukko had given her special gifts, and it was her duty to use them for her people's benefit.

In her first foray, when she was thirteen, she led a band of men who captured a border storehouse and half a dozen able slaves. In her second, an entire village fled before the screaming eagle. By the time she was sixteen, her name alone inspired fear in the southern tribes.

She lived alone with her father in a turf-covered forest tent far from the nearest farm or village. They were never cold or hungry, for petitioners came often with furs and gifts of food in exchange for divinations. Nor was she lonely, for the forest was full of spirit voices. The men and women who came to her with their foolish questions—"Should I marry this one, or that? Will my child be a son?"—she accounted a nuisance, though she did her best to find them answers.

Her father had given up the rest of his family, and considered it no sacrifice. "It would be better for you never to marry," he advised Louhi. "But if you do, it must be only for your convenience. If you have children, they must not engage your emotions. You were born to serve only Pohjola, and you must never forget it."

She never did. When her father died, she had continued to live alone in the tent. There were more battle raids, most of them successful, and her reputation was such that no one dared to molest her. She purposely cultivated a fearsome appearance, letting her nails grow long and curved, her hair hang loose and lank and tangled. A scar on her cheek, which she could have cured with herbs, she allowed to remain livid against her pale skin. She dressed always in black.

Now, staring at the wall, at Taisto's sword which she had never removed, Louhi wondered how he had ever dared to court her. Taisto had been a man of peace, for all his warlike name. He had been a soft-spoken, gentle person, and it was that mildness which had aroused something in her, which had made her plot to win him.

"Bring me your father's sword," she said to Kaisa. "And don't look so frightened—I don't intend to use it. The blacksmith is safe from me, and so is Lahja's murderer."

Kaisa complied, and Louhi held the weapon in her lap and stroked the smooth metal. No, Taisto had been no warrior, but because he had died with the sword in his hand she could feel his presence strongly when she touched it so.

Her husband's face looked up at her now, reflected in the blade. It was his young face, his open, innocent, twenty-year-old face, the one she had recognized as something from a recurring dream when he had come to her tent in the woods with the fur of a marten and a question for her to answer.

She had been ashamed of her greasy hair and unwashed body. She remembered it so vividly that she allowed the years to slip away. . . .

At twenty-five Louhi was a woman past her prime, and she knew she looked at least a decade older. For the first time she regretted it.

The young man addressed her with mingled fear and respect. His question was a simple one: he had the opportunity to buy his neighbor's farm, but he wondered if it would be wise. "I would be in debt for years," he explained. "If my crops ever failed, I would be ruined. I could lose everything."

His eyes were the clear blue of a mountain lake. And as guileless. Louhi read his nature in them, and she yearned toward it as to respite in the midst of battle. No, you mustn't ever suffer, she thought. She wanted to smooth away the tiny furrow that marred his brow, to brush back the cowlick and re-button his crooked jacket.

Instead, she retreated into the shadows of the tent wall. "What does your wife say?" she asked.

"I have no wife. I am quite alone, with both my parents gone. I can manage the small farm well enough, but the other—I just don't know. It's such an opportunity, though, with the fields adjoining . . . and if I don't buy it, someone else will."

"So you want my advice."

"If you please."

My advice is for you to marry me, she surprised herself by thinking. *I have enough riches in my chest to buy you your fields and to hire you ser-*

vants to work them. And I could have something of a life. Suddenly the dark, smoky tent was distasteful to her. So was the solitude, and—yes—the loneliness. She would never betray her first duty, but there was no reason she couldn't have some comfort, too.

The young man waited for his answer.

Louhi pushed away the drum she would have used for her seeking. She didn't want him to see her convulsed and wailing. She didn't want him to see her any longer as the hag she knew she looked. "I can't tell you today," she said. "I need to make . . . certain preparations. Can you come back in a week?"

"Of course I can." He began to back out. "The fur—is it enough?"

"Yes, yes." She was impatient for him to be gone, but called him back from the doorflap. "You didn't tell me your name."

"Taisto. From North Farm."

Taisto. War. She would marry war. The implication bothered her, but she told herself that she was already committed to a bloody cause. The young man wasn't responsible for his name, and Taisto the farmer would be her perfect mate. Earth to her fire, calm to her storm, appeasement to her fury.

When he was gone, she started at once on her physical transformation. She begged a daily sauna from her nearest neighbor, steamed herself repeatedly and washed her hair in many waters, trimmed her nails and rubbed her body with sweet oils. She made a salve of healing herbs for the scar on her face, and every night before sleeping she recited a charm to cure such injury from iron.

When Taisto came again, the scar was a barely visible thin line. She had braided her hair with red ribbons and draped a white shawl over her black-clad shoulders. At the last moment, she pinched her cheeks to bring out color.

He couldn't conceal his puzzled surprise. "You look so . . . different!"

"I was ill when you came before," she said. "It's why I sent you away."

His face cleared, then clouded again. "Are you sure you're all right now? I wouldn't want you to tire yourself on my account."

"No, I'm quite well," she said with a smile. "Don't I look it?"

"You look . . . beautiful. No one told me . . . that is, I thought. . . . " He grew red with confusion.

"That I was a fearsomely ugly creature? I can appear that way, if I choose. But this is my true form. Come closer, if you doubt it."

He did, close enough to inhale her scent. She smiled again. "I've considered your problem all week, and my advice is for you to buy the farm. It will turn out well."

"You're sure? You saw it in the fire, or on the drum?"

"I didn't need to. I saw it in your face. You'll need a helpmeet for such a large estate, but for a young man of your prospects and appearance, that shouldn't be difficult."

He shook his head. "I don't know. I can't offer much to a woman except hard work and debts."

"Perhaps you can find one with means. Maybe even a small fortune, that she would be willing to share with you."

He grimaced. "A widow long in the tooth? I'm not that desperate."

"Perhaps . . . you'll find one more agreeable. Who knows what lies in the future." She held Taisto's gaze until she modestly lowered her eyes. She had said enough. The idea was planted. Now, to nourish it. She had made the tent cozy—soft furs on the floor, a glowing log in the firepit and a rabbit roasting on a spit. "Will you stay for supper?" she asked. "I'd enjoy the company."

He agreed gladly, and just as happily accompanied her on a forest walk before the meal. They walked again afterwards, and she allowed his arm to remain around her waist. When they said farewell, his eyes were as bright and his smile as complacent as if he had already seen the contents of her treasure chest.

They were married a week later, with little ceremony. The enlarged farm prospered, and in less than a year Toini was born. Kaisa followed the next year, and then Lahja. Sweet babies, all of them, but Louhi remembered her father's admonition and entrusted them entirely to nursemaids, never allowing them to seize her heartstrings.

It was no problem with Toini and Kaisa, who were children only of her body, but Lahja . . . from the moment Louhi had looked into her newborn eyes she had recognized her as a child of her spirit.

A tear fell onto the polished blade of Taisto's sword. Louhi straightened abruptly and dabbed angrily at the betraying eye. She had lost herself too completely in the past. She had never allowed herself to weep over what she had given up, and now it was too late for regrets.

Louhi answered the accusing inner voice that she could never quite silence. She had made her choice, and who would say it had been a wrong one? Pohjola had grown strong under her leadership, and Taisto had given the children the affection they didn't receive from her.

The witch-mother saw in her mind's eye Lahja's graceful little figure as she ran screaming and laughing to her father's arms. She saw him twirl her and lift her to his shoulders, where she sat crowing with delight.

I would have done you no service to hold you close to myself, Louhi told the laughing child. I didn't want to discover my own gifts in you. I wanted to spare you my own childhood, my own life.

The child became the maiden Lahja in the blue dress, reproach in her eyes and tears on her cheeks. *You sold me*, she accused. *Was that the act of an unselfish mother?*

We needed the Sampo, Louhi defended herself. And you wanted to go with Ilmarinen. I opposed it, but you thought you loved him.

No one ever really opposed you. It was Taisto's voice, and Louhi buried her face in her hands. Of course he would come back to reproach her, too. As if she hadn't heard enough complaints during his lifetime. Couldn't she be at home more, like other wives? Surely someone else could occasionally lead a war party. And did she have to attend every council meeting? The housemaids were slovenly, and nursemaids could never take the place of a mother. And he hated having to sleep alone so often.

She had taken away his manhood, he had said at the end. Other men ridiculed him. *The witch's wife*, they called him, and Louhi couldn't silence the tongues. When Taisto heard it, he had demanded to go with the warriors on the next raid.

Of course, she had forbidden it. What would it prove to have him lose an eye or a limb? But he had seen her off coldly, and when she returned, there was no welcome for her in their bed.

What could she have done differently? She had given him his farm and his children, and shouldn't that have been enough? Her true devotion, she owed to Pohjola.

Kaisa coughed, jarring Louhi back into the present. "Are you all right, Mother?" she asked.

Louhi settled her features into an expressionless mask and uncovered her face. "Yes. I was thinking about the planting tomorrow." She saw that Kaisa had cleared and washed the table, and nodded her approval. "You can go to bed. It'll be a busy day, with hungry men to feed."

Taisto would have taken care of the planting, she thought. Even cold as he had become toward her, he hadn't neglected the farm.

But that coldness . . . it had eaten away at her. Louhi shivered and moved closer to the fire.

To remove that coldness, she had finally allowed Taisto to unsheath his sword. Louhi stared into the flames, remembering. That bloody day. . . .

The brash, swaggering lout Lemminkäinen had come to the farm spoiling for a fight. When he flung the insulting epithet at Taisto, the enraged farmer had immediately accepted the challenge.

"No, let me fight him," Louhi had begged. Taisto was no match for Lemminkäinen, even drunk as the Kalevalander was. She had tried to wrest away Taisto's sword, but he turned on her a white, furious face. "Let me fight my own battle," he had hissed. "For once, let me be a man."

She had yielded, and it had been no contest. When Taisto lay mortally wounded in her arms, she had tried to voice the words she had never dared to speak. He had stared with unseeing eyes, and she knew it was too late for such amends.

Louhi lifted the sword that still lay in her lap. "I sacrificed you as well as my daughter," she whispered to her husband's ghost. She had sacrificed her own life, too—her right to normal human affections—and to what end? Whenever she looked into the fire, into the future, she saw only war and more war. The Sampo had brought full storehouses, but because of it men were dying in greater numbers than ever before.

"Lahja," she whispered. "Taisto." Forgiveness, she didn't expect. But if only there could be a sign that they understood. Her years hung heavily on her as she rose creakily from the bench, and she walked to the door with the bent spine of an old woman.

Outside, the sky was darkening over the southern land where Lahja lay buried. Taisto's grave under the oak was splashed with gold from the setting sun, a gold that shone through a brightening wash of rose and salmon and apricot. Above the forest horizon, pale gossamer curtains of light undulated across the northern skies. Louhi watched in awe as long banners unfolded in waves of pale green and soft rose, folded back on themselves and then unfurled again. Delicate, tremulous and evanescent. Spirits dancing, with the barely audible sound of a muffled swish.

Louhi begged them for a message. She had never been able to contact Taisto, not even when the spirits danced in greatest numbers. But Lahja, who had the gift. . . .

She was almost afraid when she spotted a dark speck flying out of the forest. It grew larger, black wings stark against the shimmering light. Louhi gasped; she hadn't expected a physical form.

The eagle swooped low over the farmyard. There were no words, but as Lahja's essence met Louhi's, the mother felt in it no hate or blame. The eagle turned and glided toward the softly glowing aurora, and as it disappeared from sight Louhi was eased of her most grievous burden.

Tomorrow she would have to see the blacksmith again, and she would have to cook for an army of field workers. She might even be called to another council of war. But tonight, she owed no one a duty. Tonight, she would sleep under Taisto's tree.

Six

Mielikki

စာ ❀ ∞

"Where are you, my little daughter?
Come home now, my little girl."
The Kalevala, Runo 34

Mielikki heard the words clearly in the sound of the wind as it whistled across the open expanse of snow. *If only I could,* she thought as she pushed off, kicking with her right ski and sliding with her left. The skis were new, designed for racing, with the left a bit longer and the right strapped underneath with skin for traction. She had purchased them with the last of her housemaid wages, determined to make this journey to the Lapp soothsayer as quickly as possible.

"Such foolishness," Mielikki's former mistress had scolded. The voice Mielikki heard in her dreams at night couldn't possibly be that of her mother, still searching. After sixteen years, the lost child would have been long ago given up for dead.

Perhaps. She was probably off on a harebrained quest, Mielikki acknowledged. But all during those years she had heard the voice in her dreams, in the wind, in the rush of water and in the cries of seabirds. She could no more silence its pleading than she could cease to breathe.

She had been found by hunters, a child of three or four, wandering lost and speechless in the woods. No one in any of the villages where her rescuers made inquiry had come forth to claim her. Though she eventually began to talk again, she had been unable to tell either her name or anything about her family. The hunters, part of a roving band, called her Mielikki, after the forest spirit, and she had stayed with the tribe for three years.

Their women would have kept her longer if game had continued plentiful, but, one lean winter when their own children grew thin, they had traded her, regretfully, to a farmer's wife for a bin of corn. There, her habit of wandering off, following a voice no one else heard, led to another fosterage and then a succession of them. She had lived with a weaver's family, a woodcutter's, a fisherman's, and with several more farmers.

Most of the families had treated her well enough, but she had never been accepted as a daughter. Always an outsider, only the dream voice promised her love. When she was grown, the child Mielikki told herself, she would answer that pleading; she would find her mother.

She had tried. As a young woman adept at spinning and weaving, milking and churning and all forms of housework, she had found work easily. She had moved often, always, wherever she found herself, asking about lost children. Her present journey was her most ambitious yet. In her last position she had managed to save enough to equip her for the trip north to question the *noaide* known as Old Aslak, said to be the best interpreter of dreams and portents of any of the Lapp shamans. If anyone could help her, she thought, it would be he.

Mielikki bent low and churned the snow with her speed. The Lapp camp, so she had been told, was still half a day's journey away, and in this early winter season she was already skiing into dusk. She wasn't afraid—she'd slept in snow caves before, and she had a sharp knife in case there were predators. "Wait until spring," she had been advised, but she'd waited so long already that her urgency wouldn't be denied.

There had been too many false hopes. The woman in Pohjola who claimed to be her mother until neighbors led her to the long-dead daughter's grave. The glib-tongued wizard who had taken all of her first savings and vanished. The rumors that had led to nothing.

She remembered laughter, and being held in strong arms. She remembered a mother's soft kiss, and that was all. Perhaps she could have forgotten, and been content in whatever life she made for herself, if it hadn't been for the voice.

This would be the last attempt, she vowed. If it failed . . . so be it. She was a grown woman now, and able to marry and form her own family. Granted, she was no beauty, but her sturdy figure was strong, and her face, though broad and freckled, was not displeasing. There were plenty of young men wherever she had worked who had offered to carry her full milk pails or had loitered on wash day at the launder stones.

With the wind at her back, Mielikki made good time across the snow-covered tundra. The sun hung glowing, low on the horizon, surrounded by halos of gold and carmine and deep purple. It sank with a brilliant wash of color that reflected onto the white surface. When the colors finally faded, a full moon cast a pale light over the flat expanse, and Mielikki could see clearly enough in all directions that she wasn't uneasy. She sped on.

After several hours of steady progress the wind shifted and grew stronger, swirling the loose snow into an obscuring blanket. Mielikki pulled her fur-lined hood closer over her ears. She hoped she was on course. Even when she had been able to see, there were no guide marks. The man at the last village had merely told her to keep the sun on her right, the moon on her left, and to look out for reindeer.

According to her best estimate, she should be near her goal, but, when the wind died for a few minutes and the snow settled, she could see nothing in any direction that looked like a herder's camp. What if she had overshot it? She slowed and began to think about stopping for the night. She would be able to search better in the daylight, especially if she had to retrace her steps.

But . . . what if she were indeed very near? All that wasted time, and she knew she would be unable to sleep. *Ukko, send me a sign,* she prayed.

In answer, she heard a sound behind her, and a one-man sled pulled by a reindeer appeared out of the gray mist. "Are you going to your camp?" she shouted. She pantomimed the word, "camp," tenting her fingers.

The man in the sled motioned for her to follow him. After a half hour or so they came upon a herd of reindeer grazing on snow-covered lichen, and in another few minutes to a group of scattered tents. The fur-clad figures standing about outside stared at Mielikki curiously, but offered no welcome.

She knew little of the Lapps, only the fearsome stories told to children as warnings against misbehavior. Unsure of proper protocol, she approached the nearest figure and bowed slightly. "I am looking for Old Aslak," she said. "Is he with you?"

There were more stares, and grumblings that she couldn't understand. "Old Aslak," she repeated. "The *noaide.*"

She knew that this far north there would be a difficulty with language, but she had been told that the shaman would understand her. "Please," she begged, clasping her hands in what she hoped was a universal gesture.

One of the men grunted and pointed to the largest tent. A child scooted from between his legs and dashed ahead of Mielikki, ducking under the tent flap and then holding it open for her.

Inside, she squatted by the door, waiting to be invited farther in. She saw nothing at first but the red glow of the fire stones. Then, as her eyes adjusted, a man sitting cross-legged on the far side of the fire pit looked up at her. He had a dark, weathered face, unbearded and immensely wrinkled, with slitted eyes which held her gaze with an unnerving intensity.

The man, whom Mielikki guessed to be the shaman, spoke a single sentence in the Lapp language and indicated that she was to sit beside him.

"He says that he has been expecting you." The interpreter, a younger man, sat farther back in the shadows. The tent, Mielikki saw as she made her way around the fire to the old man's side, was otherwise empty. Like the others in the camp, it was circular, constructed of poles and skins. The floor was covered with soft hides, and above, when she looked through the open top, Mielikki could see the North Star.

The younger man wore a richly decorated tunic and cap, but the old shaman was soberly dressed in black. He sat easily, his face impassive, in an attitude of waiting.

Mielikki doffed her outer furs and sat beside him. She dug in a pocket and extracted a gold coin, which she offered with what she hoped was proper deference.

He ignored the offering, and she placed it on the ground hide beside him. "I am searching for my family," she said. "Can you help me?"

Old Aslak stared into the fire. His words came slowly, accompanied by sorrowful shakes of his head.

The interpreter translated. "There are many troubled spirits. It would be better to look no further."

Mielikki refused to consider the warning; she had come too far to be put off. "I have heard my mother call," she insisted. "I must find her."

The shaman uttered a deep sigh. After a long moment of silence, he picked up a flat, oval-shaped drum of stretched hide and placed it between his knees. The top of the drum was covered with red symbols, some recognizable as figures of humans and animals, but most strange to Mielikki's eyes. He placed a small ring on the surface of the drum, then began to beat on it with a reindeer antler while he chanted in a high, keening voice. The ring jumped about, landing on various symbols. The shaman watched intently, then abruptly ceased beating and stared again into the fire.

There was pity in his face when he turned to Mielikki, and his words, once more, seemed to come with reluctance.

The interpreter translated in an impersonal tone. "Your mother lives, and your brother. The rest are dead, and the land is gone. The man responsible is called Untamoinen, and he was your father's brother. He is known in Kaleva, but it will be ill for you if you look for any of them."

"Why? What will happen?" Hope and fear fought in Mielikki, but hope won. Her Mother! To find her at last! "Can you tell me more?" she begged.

The shaman turned his face away from her.

"Please." She turned to the interpreter, proferring another coin, but he ignored it. "You must go now," he said.

There seemed nothing for her to do but leave the tent. Outside, with no one in sight, the encampment looked more unwelcoming than ever, and Mielikki began to think she would indeed have to dig herself a snow cave for the night. She found her skis and began to strap them on when a woman came out of one of the tents and beckoned to her.

The woman conveyed by signs that she could sleep inside, and Mielikki accepted the hospitality gratefully. She shared a supper of reindeer stew with the family and then curled up on a bed of skins. She slept fitfully, trying to plan what she should do next.

Your mother lives, and your brother. The destroyer, Untamoinen, was known in Kaleva, the shaman had said. He was probably a big landowner, and all she had to do was ask around. If what Aslak said was true, she was from the same noble family. *Wealth. Nobility.* It was hard to imagine, she was so used to being ordered about, to emptying slops and scrubbing floors and turning a grindstone until her arms ached. But she would have to endure it a while longer, she told herself. She couldn't approach Untamoinen as a long-lost relative. Not with a blood feud that might still be simmering. She would have to be careful, to be devious, to swallow any thoughts of revenge until she and the remains of her family were reunited.

In the morning she headed south. In Lapland she had only to mention the name of Old Aslak to ensure a friendly reception from the few reindeer herders she encountered. In Pohjola she kept to the woods and unsettled areas. War was raging again between Pohjola and Kaleva, and Mielikki feared being recognized as a Kalevalander, particularly as a female, subject to rape and captured slavery. Unwilling to trust anyone in the witch Louhi's domain, she tightened her stomach against pangs of hunger and circled wide around every farm.

She slept in snow burrows and ate meagerly of bread and fish paste from her pack. In the woods she felt safe, as she always had. Her namesake, the Mistress of the Forest, would let no harm come to her. When she had been found by the hunters, so they told her, there had been no marks on her, no scratches, though it was the season for brambles and she had apparently been wandering for days.

Later, growing up as a serving girl, the forest spirit had comforted her when village children had mocked her or the weaver's wife had beaten her. Fleeing to the forest, she had found healing in the silent trees and grassy glades, and at times, when she listened hard, she had heard the voice of her mother in the rustling of a branch. Sometimes, too, she had imagined the forest Lady—or was it her mother?—watching her, peering between trees through a veil of moss. The Lady, dressed in a leafy green gown, was as tall and slender as the child Mielikki was short and squat. She never showed herself clearly, but Mielikki was certain she would have no freckles.

Now, the winter forest, in its silent, snow-covered beauty, was just as welcoming to Mielikki. Her guardian spirit seemed to glide before her, finding the easiest passages and showing her the most protected places for her evening camps. When she came at last upon a well-marked trail, she recognized it as one she had taken before; one that led to a village of her own people.

"Untamoinen?" Yes, the village elder, when questioned, had heard of him. "He owns practically all of Otso Province. And he's still acquiring land, by one means or another."

Bloody means, Mielikki thought. *His own brother.*

The man's eyes narrowed at something in Mielikki's expression. "I hear he's not one to have as an enemy. What do you want of him?"

I'd like his head, she thought, but aloud she said, as calmly as she could manage, "A job. I was told he pays wages, even to women."

The man shook his head doubtfully. "I don't know about that. Maybe in the south things are better, but here, with the corn blight and the Pohjolanders' raids—nobody's taking on help."

"That's why I'm traveling on," Mielikki said. She thanked the man and bought a few supplies with her last coin. She would need to find work soon, and with luck it would be in Otso Province.

*   *   *

Untamoinen's housekeeper took her on as a household drudge. The estate was large, but it looked to Mielikki to be poorly run. The manor house was cold and unkempt, with the mistress away, and the master, Untamoinen, appeared to be half drunk as he lurched about the farmyard.

Mielikki was offered no pay, stingy rations and a pallet in a drafty outbuilding. "Count yourself lucky," the sour-faced workmistress said. "Plenty are going hungry in these parts. Just remember that here it's no work, no food."

She might as well be a slave, Mielikki thought as she settled into the dawn to dusk labor. It was the worst situation she'd ever had; even at the poorest farmer's home she'd been more comfortably housed and better fed. In other circumstances she wouldn't have stayed a week, but her two fellow maids were friendly and talkative, with no love for their master. Once they had accepted her, it was easy to get information.

She didn't wait long. "Did the master really get so rich by taking his brother's land?" she asked the gossip-loving Anja while the two were fulling homespun in the storehouse shed. The young women stood facing one another, beating with their bare feet the wet cloth laid out on the floor.

Anja looked over her shoulder to check that there was no one to overhear. "Even worse than that," she said in a low voice. "He burned the homestead and killed all the family."

81

Mielikki widened her eyes. "All of them? How horrible!"

"All except one." Anja sprinkled more water on the cloth and resumed her shuffling dance. "Untamoinen spared a pregnant housemaid. Pregnant by his brother, she said, though no one knows for sure. Later he tried to raise the boy, but he turned out badly."

Mielikki's pulse quickened. Her mother and brother! It must be! But . . . a housemaid. Her dreams of nobility crumbled, but not her determination to find the two. "So what happened to the boy and his mother?" she pursued.

"I don't know about the mother—she vanished. But the boy—Kullervo, he was called—grew up to be a devil. They say he caused the death of a child he was supposed to be watching. And as for his temper—well, no one was safe around him. Untamoinen tried to tame him, but he couldn't. Couldn't get any work out of him either, so he sold him to the blacksmith Ilmarinen." Anja stopped her stamping to look around again. She lowered her voice still more. "The blacksmith's wife got eaten by a bear, and both Untamoinen and Ilmarinen swear it was Kullervo's doing. They've put a price on his head."

Mielikki tried to hide her dismay. "Then . . . where is he now?"

Anja shook her head. "Nobody knows. But good riddance, I say. He was a spawn of Hiisi if there ever was one. A monster."

The shed door creaked, and Anja put a finger to her lips. Both young women stiffened until they saw that it was the other maid, Vuokko, with a new bolt of unfulled homespun.

Vuokko looked eagerly from Anja to Mielikki. "Who are you talking about?" she asked with a giggle.

"Kullervo," Anja said. "Who do you suppose?"

"Oh, that one." Vuokko sniffed as she spread out her cloth. "There are enough stories about him to last forever."

"Did you ever see him?" Mielikki asked. "Was he really so horrible?"

"No, he was gone before I came here," Vuokko replied. "But I hear he was someone to give you nightmares. Strong as an ox, they say—could lift a man with one hand—and uglier than any Pohjolander. At least, he must have been ugly, he was so wicked. No one would have anything to do with him except the blacksmith's wife, and look what happened to her."

Mielikki's heart was a leaden weight. What a legacy to have found! But Untamoinen had probably treated the boy badly. Could he really be so evil? And what of his mother? *Her* mother. Mielikki was afraid to arouse suspicion by more questions, so she let the matter rest, for the time.

Later, questioning one of the older servants, she learned of a woman who might know of Kullervo's mother. On her half day off she skied to a small farm that bordered the woods, where she talked to a thin, worn-looking woman with a pockmarked face who regarded her with distrust.

"The mother of that wretch Kullervo? Yes, I knew her once," the woman said. "What do you want with her? The poor woman has had enough sorrow in her life. That daughter who was lost. The massacre. Thanks to the gods she never knew how her son turned out."

"That daughter. . . . " Mielikki was afraid to say more.

"They were picking berries in the woods, and the child wandered off. Simply disappeared. No trace, though we all searched for days." She studied Mielikki again, and rubbed her forehead. "There's something about you . . . you aren't . . . you couldn't be. . . .

"I think so," Mielikki said. "I think I'm that girl, and she must be my mother. I've been searching for her . . . forever. Can you tell me where she's gone?"

The woman embraced her, weeping. "What a joy! We never thought . . . but you must go to her at once!" She wiped her eyes and drew a crude map on the floor. "I don't know exactly, but I've heard she's living up near the Lapp border. About here. You follow this river through Pohjola, keeping to the west bank. I think the place is near a rapids." She put down her charcoal stick and frowned. "You won't tell anyone, will you? There are some here who would still do her harm. And you, too, if they knew who you were."

"I won't tell a soul," Mielikki promised. Especially, she thought, living where she was. She had been lucky, she realized now, that no one at the estate had seen a family resemblance.

On the way back to Untamoinen's, she planned how to get out of her contracted service. If she simply walked away, her master could keep all her belongings. Not that there were many, but she couldn't afford to lose her comb and her brush and her only change of clothing.

A sick relative, she decided. A grandmother. They would have to believe her. She had her story well rehearsed when the housekeeper met her at the farmyard gate.

"On your way, girl." The scowling woman handed Mielikki her bundle of clothing. "You're not welcome here any longer. In fact, better get as far from Otso Province as you can."

Mielikki took the bundle. "What have I done?" she asked, feigning innocence. She was fairly sure what the answer would be.

She was not mistaken. "You've been asking questions. The master doesn't welcome nosy servants. Now go, before he decides not to let you off so easily." She closed the gate with a thump of the crossbar.

Mielikki checked the bundle, and everything seemed to be there.

There was even a surprise—bread and a chunk of cheese, wrapped in her nightgown. She silently thanked Anja and Vuokko. She didn't relish the long journey back through Pohjola, but at least now she wouldn't have to beg food along the way.

She set off at once, zig-zagging through the woods in case she was followed. She glimpsed the green Lady once, pointing her away from a snow-covered windfall trap. The Lady shimmered in a last reflection of sunlight, and in a whistle of wind Mielikki heard the drawn-out syllable, "Soon."

Mielikki hoped it meant that she would soon be with her mother. However, she couldn't help remembering the *noaide*'s warning. So far, her search had been easy, and the only ill she had suffered had been losing a job she hadn't really wanted. That and the discovery of a brother whom everyone hated and feared.

No one's family was perfect, she thought as she skied into the darkening night. And the infamous Kullervo was probably far away, perhaps even across the ocean in Viroland or some such foreign place. She and her mother would never need to meet him.

She slept in a snug snow hollow beneath a sheltering oak. The next day she came to the river. It was wide, with high, snowy banks sloping to a thin layer of ice. In places Mielikki could see the dark current moving beneath the ice. Like flowing blood, she thought, and shivered and looked away.

The thinning woods on the west bank, which she was following according to her instructions, soon gave way to flat, open country. Mielikki didn't like being so exposed, but she had no choice. She tried to think of her goal, of the cabin by the river and the woman inside, of the joyful reunion. She tried to imagine her mother's face, but all she could see were the sour visages of Untamoinen's housekeeper and the weaver's wife. The wind moaned and whistled, but it no longer spoke with her mother's voice. The only voice she heard was that of Old Aslak. *It will be ill for you.*

The river followed a meandering course, almost circling in places, making the journey through Pohjola twice as long as it should have been. Mielikki's bread and cheese were gone by the third day. She ate snow and endured hunger pangs, and on the fourth day one of her ski bindings broke.

She cut a strip from her parka lining to fashion a makeshift strap, but she couldn't get it to fit tightly enough. She wobbled when she skied, and trying to work up a new pace, fell and twisted her left ankle.

She blinked tears from her eyes and cursed softly. Just when she must be so near. . . . The river stretched on, and beyond that next bend, she thought, surely must be the rapids.

She limped on, leaning heavily on her ski pole. She rounded the bend, and there were no rapids. She look behind, to see if she could have missed them, and saw a dark speck approaching over the snow plain.

It grew larger, and became a horse-pulled sleigh. A lump of fear rose in Mielikki's throat. If only she were across the river, where a piney forest came down to the water. She could hide there, with the help of the green Lady. But here, there was no escape.

The sleigh pulled up to her and stopped. The driver was a pleasant-faced young man—in appearance, at least, no ruffian—but Mielikki knew better than to trust first impressions. "You look like you're in trouble," he said. "I'm going your way, why don't you climb in and ride with me?"

"No, thank you," Mielikki said. "I'm fine, really I am." She skied on, as straight as she could, trying not to favor her throbbing ankle.

He brought the sleigh abreast of her again. "At least rest here a few minutes and let me fix that ski for you. You can't go far that way."

He didn't have the accent of a Pohjolander, and the lock of hair that fell over his forehead was as yellow as that of any southerner. Mielikki had heard enough warning stories about foolish girls who got into sleighs with strange young men, but it seemed to her it would be more foolish now to refuse. She felt for her knife, where it nestled reassuringly against her waist, and accepted his offer.

She unstrapped her skis, and he lifted her into the sleigh as easily as if she were made of feathers. Something clicked in her mind, some forgotten bit of information, but it was gone before she could retrieve it. The young man examined her ski binding and shook his head. "I haven't the tools with me here, but just tell me where you're going and I'll take you there." He clucked to his horse and they started off.

He kept the horse to a walk, and she thought, good, she could jump out at any time. He repeated his question, but she didn't trust him enough to reveal anything. "Where are you going?" she countered.

"Home." He grinned. "I've just been to the village to pay my taxes." He held up a flat leather pouch, jingling whatever remained in the bottom. Something in his expression changed, a look she didn't like at all, as he poured the few coins into her lap. "There's just enough left to buy me something, and you could earn it easily. What do you say?" With his face so close to hers, she could smell the drink on his breath. His hand, which he tried to force into the opening of her parka, left no doubt as to his intentions.

She found her knife and pulled it out, knicking his hand with the blade. "I say you'd better let me go!"

He gave a roar of rage and knocked the knife from her hand. "Nobody cuts me!" he bellowed. He forced Mielikki easily down to the floor of the sleigh, straddling her and tearing away the layers of her furs. He was immensely strong, so strong that her struggles were useless. She cried out when he thrust into her, the pain and the violation tearing her, tearing both her flesh and her spirit.

She stared up at him dumbly when he was finished. "You can have the money," he said, as remorseless as if she had agreed to the act. "And I *will* fix your ski. Now tell me where it is you're going."

Mielikki sat up and tried to rearrange her clothing. Her undershift was sticky with blood, and she hurt when she moved. "I'm on my way to my family," she said, her voice choking with her bitterness. "I have a brother who will probably kill you."

He shrugged. "Not very likely."

Had he no human feelings? "Do *you* have a sister?" she ventured.

He stared into the distance. "I did once. Or so my mother says. I never knew her."

Mielikki stopped breathing. *It couldn't be.* She sat frozen, dreading what she didn't dare think.

He went on, oblivious to her distress. "She wandered away before I was born. Got lost in the woods. Then the rest of the family was wiped out. Butchered. I only found my mother again recently."

Mielikki heard the words in a dark fog of horror. She feared to hear more, yet she had to be certain. "What . . . why were they killed?"

His face became stone. "A feud between brothers. I only live to avenge myself on my uncle."

There was no doubt, now. "What was your father's name?" she whispered.

"Kalervo."

"And your name?"

"Kullervo Kalervoson."

The world swam, and when it had settled and she could breathe again, Kullervo was urging his horse to a faster pace. She cried, "Stop!" and when he didn't respond, seized his arm. "This is as far as I can go." She swung a leg over the side of the sleigh. "Stop, and let me out here."

"Are you crazy?" he said, but he obediently slowed. "There's nothing here. My mother's house is just past those rapids." He pointed ahead. "She'll take you in, if you've nowhere to go."

"It's too late." Mielikki leaped from the sleigh. "I was on my way to that very house, but now it's too late."

Kullervo leaned down to reach for her, but she moved away. "I don't understand," he said. "I've not seen you in these parts before."

She started for the river. "I was going home," she shouted back over her shoulder. "For the first time. You must tell your mother what you've done to her lost child."

There was no answer and no pursuit. Mielikki didn't look back; she couldn't bear the sight of him, the thought of him. She couldn't bear the thought of life itself, and the river was so near. Perhaps the dark water would cleanse her, wash away her shame.

She trudged through the knee-deep snow, feeling no pain from her ankle; feeling nothing. She slid down the bank and her feet broke easily through the layer of ice. As she waded out, the water soaked her furs and their weight pulled her down. She suffered a moment of fear before she submerged, but it was gone when the Lady appeared on the far bank and held out her arms. She knew then that truly she was going home.

Seven

The Mother

"What has happened now, my son,
What strange wonder to be heard?
You look as if you came from Tuoni,
As if risen from the grave."

The Kalevala, Runo 35

I knew as soon as I saw him that Kullervo had done something terrible. He'd been drinking, and with his temper it could have been anything. He had abandoned his sleigh and come galloping home, his horse in a froth and his eyes as wild as if he had escaped all the terrors of Tuonela.

I tried to prepare myself. I'd stood by him before, in that business about the Lapp herder's daughter. And I'd hidden him when the blacksmith came from Ilma seeking vengeance. The boy had promised to settle down, to farm my rocky hillside and look after my skinny cow, and it was such a miracle to have him with me that I'd have lied myself blue to protect him.

He was so young, I never could believe all the stories about him. And if he'd paid people back ill for mistreating him, just look at the way he'd been brought up by that brute Untamoinen.

Anyway, it was easy for me to find excuses for him. But now, I thought, maybe I'd been too trusting, sending him to town with the tax money. But I couldn't go, not with my knees as bad as they get every winter, and as I said, the boy had promised to behave. So when he came home in such a state . . . I didn't need my second sight to predict that there was big trouble ahead.

At first I couldn't get anything sensible from him. "Why was I ever born?" he raved, tearing his hair. "You should have strangled me before I drew a breath! Drowned me! Burned me in my cradle!"

I grabbed his arm when he reached to take his sword from the wall. "Wait," I begged. "No more fighting. Not now." I'd bound up too many sword wounds in my time to want to go through it again. "Whatever happened, can't you solve it without a battle?" He left the sword where it hung but continued to stare wildly and moan. "I meant to use it on myself," he said. "Better to end it all now. After what I did, I don't deserve to live."

I led him to the fire and made him sit beside me on the bench. He was trembling, and I rubbed his cold hands. "Tell me about it or not, as you wish," I said. "But no more talk of killing yourself. It would mean my death, too, and do you want that on your soul?"

"It wouldn't matter, now. Nothing matters. It would be better if our line all perished."

I couldn't abide that kind of talk. Better, indeed! If I believed that, I'd never have struggled to keep myself alive all these years. It was the thought of my son, my healthy, strong baby, that had kept me going after Untamoinen banished me. That and the forlorn hope that my lost daughter might turn up some time and we would be a family again.

If Kullervo could only survive to manhood. Only sixteen, he was bigger than most men, and he had never learned to control his hot blood. I suspected that his latest misadventure concerned a woman—too many of them did—and when I asked, his answering groans told me I'd guessed right.

"I didn't know." He buried his face in his hands. "How was I to know she was my sister?"

I was struck dumb, and when he told how he had raped her and then watched her drown, I added my groans to his.

"I knew you would hate me," he said. "You were the only one in the world who didn't, and now . . . I don't know why I'm sitting here. I ought to end it the way she did, in the river." He rose, heading resolutely for the door.

I suppose I did hate him then, but what good would his death do? There had already been so many. . . . I called him back, and he obeyed. "Our whole family is accursed," I said. "And you the most of all." I couldn't bear to look at him, to hear his voice. I wanted to beat him with my fists, the way he stood there as if awaiting my judgment. Instead, I tore at my own hair and howled.

"I don't deserve to live," he said again.

I didn't dispute it, but neither would I give him permission to drown himself. My first anguish was spent, and I stared at him dully. "Perhaps you should live with your remorse," I said. "I can't forgive you now, but maybe . . . if you go away for a time, do penance in some isolated spot. . . . "

He shook his head. "I don't expect forgiveness, ever." His voice was hard, his face set in bitter lines. "We *are* accursed," he agreed. "While the one responsible grows fatter and richer every year." He clenched his fists until his knuckles showed white. "The only reason I won't follow my sister now is to ensure that my uncle gets the fate he deserves."

I protested, though I knew it was useless. All winter Kullervo had been recruiting a band of fierce-minded Pohjolanders, and they would need little urging to raid a rich farm like Untamoinen's.

Kullervo, I knew, had more in mind than plunder. I remembered the raid that had destroyed his father's and my home—the mailed warriors with their slashing swords, the screams and the blood and the buildings all in flames. I saw it happening again when I looked into Kullervo's eyes, gleaming with the lust of battle.

He gathered his gear and left while it was still light. I knew I would never see him again, and I tried to put him out of my mind, to forget that he had ever come back to me. It was the only way to escape despair.

Sometimes it works for a whole day. I feed my cow and milk her, I cook porridge for myself and tend my fire and empty my slops, and it's as though this has always been my life. I know it will never change, week after empty week. With nothing now to look forward to, I am more than ready to cross the death-dark river.

Life here in this bleak north is a never-ending winter. You barely get thawed out before it's on you again. Chilblains and coughs and aching joints. The darkness outside and the smoky fire within: the fire that, no matter how I feed it, can never warm this drafty cabin.

Kullervo should have rechinked the walls this fall, but he was too busy gathering his army.

Men! Unlike us, they love the winter. It's their time to play at warriors, neighbor against neighbor and country against country. Any excuse for a quarrel so they can sharpen their swords and march and rape and come home with a few paltry skins and tin ornaments and expect us to make over them as if they were heroes.

Even when I was younger I hated the winter. Confined to my cabin-prison, my man always after me to lie with him, any hour of the day, because when he wasn't at war he had too much time on his hands. And when he was gone, the loneliness and the fear that he wouldn't return, or that he would come back maimed in body or spirit.

My first man didn't return. In my grief I miscarried a baby, and because I was too sick to work the farm, I lost it as well. I hired out to Kalervo, Kullervo's father, as a dairymaid. Kalervo's wife was a cold-eyed shrew who gave him little comfort, and when he sought it from me I didn't turn him away. He promised to look after me and our children. There was a daughter—the one who was lost—and I was big-bellied with Kullervo when Untamoinen came with his battle-hungry raiders and destroyed everything.

I managed to escape into the woods. When Untamoinen found me, his blood had cooled enough to allow me to live. He kept the baby, but his wife didn't want me around, and I was sent away.

I've had other men since, but never any more children. Men . . . you can't depend on them. There was always a wife, or a mother who didn't think

I was good enough. Each time I moved, it was farther north.

How I wished for my son! A daughter will go to her husband's house, but a son will always care for his mother. Ilmatar knew this, when she gave birth to Väinämöinen. So did Lemminkäinen's mother, or why else would she have journeyed to Tuonela to save him?

Those women would understand why I took Kullervo in so joyfully, in spite of his reputation. They wouldn't blame me for cosseting him and protecting him. For sixteen years I had dreamt about him, longed for him. He had his father's yellow hair and his same crooked smile. I forgave him all his misdeeds and thought I always would.

Until now. This time, when he buckled on his mail and asked for my blessing, I pretended not to hear. It wasn't that Untamoinen didn't deserve his fate—I'd heard from Kullervo how he'd beaten and starved the boy, and I'd seen with my own eyes the massacre on Kalervo's farm. But I knew how it would end, in another bloody heap of bodies, and I was sick of all that.

What is wrong with men that they love war so much? My first husband left a thriving farm to go raiding. Kullervo, if he hated working the land, could have hired out on a fishing boat or as a herdsman. In every trade except war men can prosper. In war they die.

So Kullervo left me, as all the others had done. I think now, maybe my daughter would have been different. Maybe she would have been ugly and no man would have wanted her. Maybe she would have stayed here with me, and we could have chinked the cabin ourselves and it would have been snug and warm. We could have spun and sewed together and talked on these winter evenings, and they wouldn't have seemed so long.

When I think on it too much, my eyes mist. I have no tears; I am beyond all that. At such times I see with an inner eye: Kullervo, dead on his own sword, and my daughter, clothed in green, walking in the forest.

It was in the forest that I lost her. It was summer, a warm, sun-kissed day, and we had gone to gather berries. I left my Ruusuke, my little rose, in the middle of a clearing with her own moss-lined strawberry basket. There was nothing around that could harm her, only soft grass and the ground-hugging berries, and I could see her easily from the nearby bushes where I was filling my milk pail with hardier, pricklier raspberries.

I quickly picked around the edges of the clearing, but my pail was only half filled. Ruusuke was occupying herself happily, and I went deeper into the bushes, then still deeper. When I could no longer see the child, I wasn't worried. She was safe in her grassy meadow, and I occasionally called to her, and she answered.

When she didn't answer, I wasn't worried, either. She could easily have fallen asleep in the sun, and there was no need to tramp back just to look. My pail was nearly full, and I could already smell the fruit soup bubbling in the hearth kettle.

I returned to the clearing, and she wasn't there. I still didn't panic. She could have gotten too hot, I thought, and looked for shade for her nap. She couldn't be far—she was barefoot and wearing only a smock.

A path led into a grove of alders, but Ruusuke wasn't there. I called and got no answer. I found her strawberry basket where the big trees started, where the sun barely penetrated the green gloom.

By then I was frantic. I thought of bears and wolves and sinkholes. I ran this way and that, crashing through underbrush and slogging knee-deep through swamps, shouting until my throat was raw. When darkness drove me home, I clung to the one hope left to me—that she would have found her way there, that she would be waiting at our tiny cabin.

Of course, it wasn't so. Kalervo organized search parties, and they combed the woods for three days before they gave it up.

Naturally, I was blamed. Kalervo's wife said it was my punishment for bearing a bastard child. She would have prevailed on him to get rid of me if I hadn't been pregnant again.

I blamed myself, too. For weeks I promised my very soul to the forest gods if they would return my child. I swore to them that I would lead a blameless life, that I would forsake Kalervo and all other men, that I would devote myself only to my children.

The gods didn't hear me. They never have. When I lost Kullervo, too, I stopped believing in them. When he came back, for a little while, I almost believed again, but now I know that nothing has really changed.

Kullervo didn't have to rape the girl. And he wasn't sorry about it—only that she happened to have been his sister.

They say that a man will look after his mother. He's also supposed to take care of his sister. I know now that it isn't true, that a man thinks only of himself. All of us . . . we've only ourselves. Here I am, an old woman in winter in a drafty cabin, and I am tired of looking after myself. Before the snow is gone—I have seen it—I will join my Ruusuke.

Eight

Marjatta

֍ ✿ ֎

Marjatta, the beautiful,
For a long time grew at home
In her high-born father's house,
In her loving mother's chambers.

The Kalevala, runo 50

Marjatta the beautiful . . . beautiful . . . beautiful. As Marjatta knelt by the stream, Väinämöinen's words at her sister's wedding feast echoed in her mind, mocking. The old spellsinger had only been trying to please her father, Marjatta knew, but his ineptly flattering description had brought smiles to the faces of the other guests and a flood of embarrassment to hers.

Beautiful, indeed! Her reflection in the water told Marjatta the truth, and she felt the familiar bitterness. Even in the semi-concealing ripples she could see the bulging white dome of her forehead and her jutting prow of a nose. "A queenly look," her mother tried to convince her, but Marjatta knew better. No queen would willingly lay claim to such features, nor to the beady eyes half hidden under their heavy lids or the wiry hair that would never lie smooth in its braid but stood up in hay wisps all over her head.

In the water's movement the wisps waved like snakes. Marjatta shuddered, gathered her skirt around her and rose from the stream bank.

Beyond the copse of alders that edged the stream stretched the summer sheep pasture of her father's farm, the close-cropped grass rolling in gentle hills and hollows to the higher, forested slopes that rimmed it in all directions. The sheep were clustered in one of the hollows—Marjatta had checked on them earlier—and she was free to enjoy her lunch and to dream away the afternoon.

She didn't mind the lonely life of a shepherdess. Her mother had objected strongly when Marjatta had first offered to spend the summer months at the sheepherder's hut in the upland meadow. "A girl alone, all that time! Impossible!" she had exclaimed, but Marjatta had coaxed and pleaded, even cried a little, and the tears had finally won her the day. That, and her father's disgust with the shiftless youths who had held the job before.

"At least, the girl can count," her father had said. "Unlike that last addle-pate who brought the flock back with three lambs and a ewe missing, and didn't even know it."

In her three summers as a shepherdess, Marjatta hadn't lost a single animal. She saw them safely penned every night, and during the day she was never far from where they grazed. She avoided the deep woods where bears were said to lurk, and, in case one ventured into the meadow, she practiced each day throwing her spear into a tree.

So far she had never had to use the skill. Sometimes during the short hours of darkness she heard wolves and lit fires around the pen, but during the day she wandered freely and unafraid. This year, especially, she welcomed the solitude after all the noise and revelry of the wedding. What a relief it was not to have to wear a continual smile, not to force herself to laugh off the teasing, pointed remarks about "when was it going to be her turn?"

Her turn. It had long since passed, Marjatta could have told everyone. At twenty-six, she was well out of the running. As if she had ever been pursued. With her three younger sisters now married, she saw her future roles clearly: spinster aunt, her mother's housekeeper, her father's farm hand. She would care for her parents when they grew infirm, then wither up herself until she became the neighborhood crone—an old woman living alone, talking to herself and suspicious of visitors, a figure of laughter and sometimes fear to children.

She would always have a home, so she supposed she had no real cause for complaint, but it was not a future she anticipated with joy. It was certainly not the future she had imagined when she was eight and nine, loving with a fierce tenderness the newborn lambs and the barn kittens and her mother's newest baby. Or when she was ten, nursing her doll and playing mother to it and to her sisters. She hadn't known then that she was ugly, too ugly to be a wife and mother. The realization, when it came, when Helvi and Kerttu and even little Aulikki braided their hair with ribbons and acquired bashful suitors, was still a soreness in her heart that she didn't like to probe. For her there had been no one but old Jaako, who looked at least a hundred and was seeking more a nurse than a wife. Luckily, Marjatta's father, who would have liked nothing better than to see her safely married, had sent him away in short order.

Yes, this last wedding had been a trial, Marjatta thought, but thankfully it was over. Now she could hide for three months and suffer no more humiliations. The sheep didn't care about the size of her nose, and neither did the grass or the trees or the soft summer breezes. She loosened her hair and let it blow, and kicked off her shoes as well.

94

Ah, freedom! A sheep's bell tinkled, and Marjatta ran to check on her charges once more. She counted, and they were all in sight, the lambs playing on a ridge and the older animals still grazing contentedly in the hollow. She turned back to the stream, chewing the last of her bread and cheese as she brushed through the leafy alder branches. She knew where a patch of lingonberries grew in the dappled shade, and their tart sweetness was just what she needed to finish off her meal.

She found the spot, but disappointingly, the berries were still green. No, she spotted a red one high on a branch, and then another. She reached, captured the branch and popped the berry into her mouth.

It was a bit sour, but she was still hungry and ate all she could find. She was sorry an hour later when her stomach began to hurt. Why had she been so greedy? Now, as she grimaced in pain, she feared her afternoon was spoiled.

The cramp passed, however, and she relaxed upon the smooth, sun-warmed boulder where she sat with the lambs on their stony ridge. Every year she made pets of them, to her father's disgust. One, with a black nose, sniffed her curiously, and she sat very still. Soon it would know her, and even lie in her lap. She thought of a name for it—little nosy—and whispered it softly.

How could she ever be lonely? A song bird warbled from a thicket of bracken, and a snake sunned itself on a patch of bare ground. When she looked up, to the dark stand of firs on the mountain slope, Marjatta fancied the forest god Tapio looking down on her. He was smiling, she was sure—yesterday she had left him mead and honey cakes, as she did at the beginning of each summer.

Marjatta's perch on the rock was a favorite one, a spot that allowed her a sweeping vista of meadow and forest—even, through a break in the trees, to the sheep pastures of their nearest neighbor, one-eyed Ruotus.

Ruotus' shepherd waved, and Marjatta raised her own arm in reply. She was surprised at the friendly gesture. Usually Ruotus' sheepherders ignored her, knowing that she was the daughter of Sedgebrook Farm and—or so she guessed—intimidated by her father's wealth and reputation. Perhaps this was a new boy, who hadn't yet heard that the master of Sedgebrook had half killed youths who had dared to make improper advances to his younger daughters.

No danger of that with her, Marjatta thought as she returned the wave. Her mother needn't have worried about her honor—on that score she was as safe on the mountain as she would have been at home.

Another cramp attacked her suddenly, doubling her over on the rock. Again it passed, but the sun, which had been so pleasant, was now too hot. It beat down on her fiercely, giving her a headache. Her limbs ached, too, and when she arose she swayed dizzily.

She'd better get to her bed, she decided. It couldn't be anything serious—just an upset stomach. A short rest, out of the sun, and she would be all right. The hut where she slept wasn't far, just down the ridge and into the next hollow. If only the ground would stop tipping. . . . She stumbled, found a dead branch walking stick and made her faltering way.

The low, sod-roofed shelter was dark and blessedly cool. Marjatta collapsed on her pallet bed and gave herself up to her illness.

Hours passed—how many, she didn't know. Whenever she opened her eyes and tried to get up, her weakness and nausea forced her back down on the straw. Soon it was nighttime black in the hut, and she knew she should have brought in the sheep, but she couldn't move. She sank into oblivion.

She was walking in the woods, lost and afraid. Thorny underbrush snagged her clothing, and vines entangled her legs. Somewhere in the distance she heard a crashing, and she smelled the rank scent of bear. She tried to scream, but her throat closed. She tried to run, but she was held fast.

The trees parted, and Tapio stood before her. The forest god wore green, leafy clothing and a hat of fir twigs. His hair and skin and beard gleamed golden in the dark shade. With a touch he untangled the vines that bound her, and another touch cooled her fevered brow.

When she awoke, someone held a cup to her lips. She drank thirstily, but when she tried to sit up the room still spun. "Not yet," a voice said, and she closed her eyes and slept some more.

Tapio was with her again. This time they walked an acorn-strewn path through a grove of giant evergreens. His arm was around her waist, and it was strong and his skin was smooth. He was smooth all over, and cool, while she was burning. When he touched her, her fever seemed to be concentrated into one large wave within her.

Something was happening, that she thought she should stop, but couldn't. Her body felt strangely unfamiliar, as it did sometimes at night when she had similar, embarrassing dreams. She woke with a start, and it was daylight and a stranger was crouched by her pallet, holding her hand. He wore a green shirt and his hair and wispy beard were a pale flaxen, but the shirt was tattered and dirty and the hand was work roughened. He was certainly no Tapio.

Marjatta jerked her own hand free. "Who are you?" she whispered, her throat too swollen to speak clearly. "What are you doing here?" She tried to rise. "My sheep," she croaked. "I must—"

"I've seen to your sheep," he said. "That's why I came to find out what had happened to you. When I spotted your flock wandering last night, I thought something might be wrong.

"I'm Mikko," he said in answer to her first question. "Ruotus' shepherd. I waved to you yesterday, remember?"

She did—the one who hadn't known her. She sipped at the water he offered her, and the constriction in her throat eased. "You must be new around here," she said.

"Yes," he acknowledged. "I come from Pohjola, but I hurt my leg in the last fighting. I had enough of that, and wanted to get away."

Marjatta nodded. It seemed to her that the war over the Sampo had gone on forever, and she could understand his desire to escape it. "Does Ruotus know?" she asked. At Sedgebrook, her father, with all his hatred, would never hire a Pohjolander.

"I don't think so," he said. "He needed a shepherd, and didn't ask many questions."

The youth, with his downy beard and shy smile, looked too young to have been a warrior. Though in the dim light of the cave-like room, it was hard to tell. She would have liked to see him better, to dispel that troubling confusion about Tapio, but the advantage was that he couldn't see her well, either. Perhaps that was why he had been so kind.

Too kind. It was time she released him from any obligation he might feel. "I'm grateful," she said. "But you can go now. You have your work to attend to."

When he didn't move, she tried to stand. "You see, I'm quite well now."

Her legs crumpled, and he caught her as she fell. "I won't leave you," he said.

"But . . . the sheep. . . . "

"Don't worry, I'll look after both flocks," he assured her.

She was too helpless to protest. He stayed with her through the day, covering her with a blanket when she shivered and bathing her face and hands when the fever returned. He favored one foot when he walked about in the hut, but his movements were nimble, and his hands, for all their roughness, were gentle. He fed her gruel and emptied her slops, and when her head ached he stroked her hair.

"Don't," she protested, more embarrassed than offended. "It's such awful hair. Like dry hay."

"I like the way it feels," he said.

He said other things, wonderful things, when he returned from penning the sheep for the night. Or perhaps it was Tapio who said them. In her fever sleep, Marjatta couldn't distinguish between dreams and reality. Sometimes she heard her own voice, and it seemed to come from someone else. Sometimes she let Tapio stroke her hair, and it was as soft and smooth as his own. Whenever she looked into his water-green eyes, she had no will but his. She let him lead her where he would, and the woman in the dreams did not protest. He seemed to touch something in her that had been all knotted up, and now it unraveled. She only knew that she was happy, happier than she had ever been, and, when she awoke at last free from fever, it was almost with regret that she returned to her own body.

She felt sore and rumpled and smelly, but her head was mercifully clear. She was alone in the hut, and there was no sign that anyone had been there. She went to the doorway and saw Mikko coming limping across the field.

It had rained during the night. Wreaths of mist drifted about the mountainsides, and tiny streams rushed down the grassy slopes of the higher meadows. The sky was bright blue; the few clouds promised fair weather.

Marjatta wished she could appear as fresh. She washed her face in the rain barrel and started to undo her tangled braid, but gave it up when she saw the shepherd break into an awkward run.

She retreated into the safe darkness of the hut. When he appeared in the doorway, panting, she stayed in the farthest corner.

"You're better! I knew it would be so!" he exclaimed. "The summer sickness never lasts longer than two days."

"Has it been that long?" Marjatta wondered aloud. She had lost all track of time. "I don't remember much," she said. "Except that you tended me and watched my sheep as well. I owe you more thanks than I can say. My father—"

"As for that, I've had my thanks," he said. He came closer. "Why are you hiding in the corner? There's no need to be so shy with me now that you're well."

She brushed past his outstretched hands. Whatever possessed him to be so familiar? She might as well let him see her clearly and know who she was before he plunged recklessly into more danger. "Come outside," she said.

In the sunlight, she looked him straight in the face. "Now, do you know me?" She clenched her hands behind her back, expecting dismay, repulsion, maybe even fear.

He only looked puzzled. "No, not even your name," he said. "What may I call you?"

She stood straighter. "Marjatta, Olaf's daughter. Marjatta of Sedgebrook."

"The daughter of Sedgebrook!" He stepped back, his face suddenly pale. "I heard about your father, but I . . . I thought you were just a shepherdess. . . . I thought. . . ." He looked about wildly. "Ukko protect me, or I'm a dead man!" He turned and ran.

He stumbled in his haste to get away, and never once looked back. Marjatta watched him go with swimming eyes. Just for a moment, she had thought he might be different. . . .

"Foolish girl, what did you expect?" she scolded herself. And why should she care? He was only a poor shepherd, years younger than herself, without even a good shirt to his name. Granted, he had been kind, but she would never see him again and it was probably for the best.

Marjatta kept close to the hut for the next few days, not yet trusting her recovery. When she finally sat again on the viewpoint boulder, she saw a new shepherd with Ruotus' flock. This one was fat and dark-bearded, and he didn't glance once in her direction.

So Mikko had kept on running. Marjatta bit her lip and vowed to think of him no more. She had three months of peace and solitude before her; three months of almost endless days to wander the meadows and wade in the streams. She would plant a potato garden, pick wildflowers and fish in the pool below the waterfall. She would embroider a collar for little Nosy, with tinkling bells, so she would always know where he was. It had been enough for her before and would be again.

The weeks passed quietly for Marjatta, one day much like the others. Midsummer came, and she thought of the fires and the dancing and felt only thankfulness that she wasn't standing stiffly, hopelessly, on the sidelines as she had done so often. She made her own fire on the ridge, a signal to her father that she was well, but it wasn't as large as she had intended. Gathering dry branches in the morning, she had felt suddenly queasy. The illness passed after an hour, but Marjatta had feared a recurrence of the summer sickness and taken it easy for the rest of the day.

The next morning she threw up her breakfast porridge, and after that she couldn't abide even the thought of it. The smell of cheese set her stomach to heaving, too, and for days she lived on dry bread and water.

It wasn't the summer sickness. For that she still blamed the lingonberries, and she had eaten no more of them. It was a thickening of the blood, she thought, for due to her illness she had missed her monthly course. A leech-woman would have bled her, but she was afraid to open her own vein. She learned to sit quietly until the spells passed, and to eat sparingly.

She grew thin, and often she fell to weeping without any cause. She hated her weakness and the way it was ruining her summer, but she could do nothing about it. She tried to concentrate on familiar tasks, but nothing was as before. Her potato patch grew weedy, and it didn't seem to matter. The rotting post in the sheep pen fence was a more serious concern, and the morning after it collapsed she promised herself to fix it that very day. Perhaps after she caught a fish for supper. . . .

At the fishing pool, Marjatta clambered down a mud bank into a steep-sided basin. At one end, a silver curtain of water fell from a cliff to splash in a torrent of foam on the rocks below. Settled on one of the rocks across from the cataract, Marjatta stared at the continuously falling sheets, at the endless, driving, eternal force that could never be stopped, and felt herself grow as insubstantial as the mist that surrounded the waterfall. She allowed her fishing net to drop from her nerveless fingers, and as she leaned over to retrieve it, a face looked up at her from the dark water.

It wasn't her own. The eyes were large and sea green. Forest green. "Tapio," Marjatta whispered. She lifted her gaze to the opposite bank, and at first she saw nothing but the bushes, the rocks and the foam. Then, looking higher, behind the curtain of water she discerned the outline of a figure.

It hurt her eyes to look at him, and something told her it was forbidden. She turned back to the reflection in the pool.

The face wavered as he spoke. There was no sound, but Marjatta heard the words clearly in her mind. *The child will be a king. Greater than any of us.*

The face in the water sank to the bottom and disappeared. When Marjatta looked up, at the waterfall, there was no one there.

A child, he had said. Marjatta pressed a hand to her stomach, and she knew it was true. The lingonberries, she thought. Tapio's seed. She was to bear a child.

She knew a moment of pure happiness before the reality of her situation came crashing down upon her. Then, she knew nothing but fear. What was she to do? She had no husband, not even a human lover. No one to protect her. What would she tell people?—A lingonberry? Tapio? Who would believe such a fantastic story?

Certainly not her father, with his distrust of anything unfamiliar, his pride and his strict code of honor. Or her mother, who had continually exhorted her daughters to guard with their lives their "most precious treasure." Marjatta thought of the dairymaid Ilsa, whom her father had driven from the farm when she wouldn't name her seducer. She thought of the mouldy-haired man they called Risto the bastard, who butchered pigs and counted himself lucky to find a bed in a stable. What a future for her and her child!

Marjatta moaned and pressed her stomach again. Surely, the forest god would have a way to help her. "What shall I do?" she demanded of the water and the trees, but there was no answer. She asked it again, of the waterfall, but the splashing curtain revealed nothing.

Did it mean Tapio had abandoned her? "A king," he had said. Marjatta wanted desperately to believe in the prediction. With such a father, it would certainly be an extraordinary child. She closed her eyes, imagining a golden-skinned infant, and for all her troubles, already she loved it.

Perhaps the newborn child would be so beautiful that everyone would know it was god-given. Marjatta seized on the thought as to a lifeline. Yes, she told herself, it was Tapio's answer: the baby, when it came, would reveal everything.

Until then, Tapio would want her to be brave. And she could do it. She had only to endure the months of waiting; to disguise her condition as long as she could.

Marjatta returned to her hut with no fish but with a determination to make the best use of her remaining time in the mountains. No more moping about; not with the precious burden she had to protect. She was so dependent on her father's good will, she couldn't afford to let him think her slothful or inattentive to her duties.

She chopped down a green sapling for the new post, skinned it and set it securely in place. She weeded her potatoes, repaired the roof of her hut and moved the sheep to a new, lusher pasture.

Her father would have to be pleased with her, she thought. So pleased, perhaps, that when he learned of her condition. . . .

There, her hopeful projections always came to an end. Marjatta couldn't imagine telling him. Her stomach quailed even thinking about it.

Anyway, she calmed herself, the revelation was still a long way off.

By the end of the summer Marjatta's waistbands were a bit tight, but when she let them out the change in her figure was not noticeable. Her sick spells were gone, and she felt strong and healthy. She enjoyed the fall crispness in the shortening days, but at night, in the dirt-floored hut, she shivered under her furs. In the hours of darkness all the perils of her position came home to her; all the frightening possibilities. She imagined her mother's tears, her sisters' smirks, the finger-pointing gossip of the neighbors. She would have run away then if she had had a place to go. But there would be snow soon, and she was more afraid of being alone and homeless in the winter than she was of facing her father. When he finally came for her and the sheep, she was packed and as ready as she could make herself.

Olaf of Sedgebrook rode his black stallion and led Marjatta's smaller roan mare. Seated on his great horse, Olaf was an imposing presence. He rode straight-backed, controlling his mount with a mere twitch of his powerful legs. Dismounted, he was equally impressive, with the stature and breadth of a forest fir. His iron-gray hair and beard were full and bushy, his nose was as commanding as Marjatta's, and his shaggy-browed eyes lowered themselves to no one. Marjatta had always more feared than loved him.

Together, on horseback, they rounded up the sheep for the drive down the mountain. "They look good," Olaf said, counting them and nodding with approval. He noted the repaired fence and the new turf on the roof of the hut. "You've done well, as usual."

It was high praise from the usually taciturn farm master. He even bestowed a faint smile on Marjatta. "You may not have beauty, my girl, but at least you're dependable." He gazed across the hills and valleys to where his neighbor's fields lay. "Unlike poor Ruotus' shepherds."

Marjatta stiffened in her saddle, but tried to keep her voice steady. "Why—what happened over there?"

Olaf barked a laugh. "The old sod's no judge of men. The first one he hired ran off, without a by-your-leave. Sent word by a passing trapper, and simply disappeared. The second, I hear, was always drunk and lost half the flock." He favored Marjatta with another wry smile. "Yes, I count myself lucky. Now, if only you were a man. . . . "

Marjatta didn't answer. She'd heard him say it before, and what possible response could there be? Should she tell him she was sorry that she wasn't a son and heir? That she wasn't beautiful? All her life she had felt his disappointment. Maybe he was grateful to her now, as he would have been to a loyal worker, but if he knew her secret. . . . She shuddered and drew her riding cloak closely around her.

They drove the sheep down in silence, the first part of their journey a gentle descent through the valleys. When they came to forested slopes, they herded their charges along animal paths between the thick trees. In one place they clattered over stones as they descended a dark, narrow gorge, and the frightened animals set up a pitiful chorus of baa-ing. Marjatta watched out for nosy, that he wouldn't fall, and didn't breathe easily again until they emerged on to the broad, sunlit fields of Sedgebrook Farm.

They left the sheep in a fenced-in meadow. A dirt road led up to the farmyard gate, where a tangle of barking dogs welcomed them. They left their horses with the stable boy, and Olaf silenced the dogs with a single command. Marjatta reached out to pet her favorite, a droop-eared hound, but desisted at her father's frown.

"Go on to the house," Olaf said. "Show your mother that you haven't been eaten by wolves. You know how she always worries."

Marjatta sucked in her stomach as she walked past the storehouses and work sheds along the houseyard path. She had heard somewhere that a woman could always tell when another was pregnant, even if she didn't show. Something in the eyes; in the expression. Marjatta steeled her face, too, as she approached the square log manor house.

Her mother met her at the door. "Marjatta! At last! I tried to get your father to go for you sooner, but you know how he is. He had to get the corn in, and then one of the cows was sick. But look at you"—she loosened her embrace to study Marjatta. "Why the fierce look—aren't you glad to be home?"

Marjatta relaxed. "Of course I am, Mother." She gazed around the familiar room, the smoke-darkened walls adorned with her father's weapons, the warm hearth where a kettle of stew bubbled, the well-scrubbed floor and benches and table, and she felt warm, too, and for the moment, safe.

"Good. I'm glad, as well," her mother said. "I wish you'd give up that sheepherding business. It's no work for a woman, and now that your sisters are all gone there's plenty for you to do here in the summer. And look at your face—so brown! I told you to stay in the shade; your complexion is ruined. How do you ever expect—"

Marjatta stopped her. "I don't. I don't expect to get a husband." She thought of the forest god, who had chosen her, and of the seed she carried, and bit her lip to keep from blurting it out.

Her mother had once seen the Moonmaid, on Midsummer's Eve, and talked with her. If it weren't for Olaf, Marjatta thought, her mother might believe what had happened to her daughter. But the master of Sedgebrook held that only Pohjolanders had truck with the spirit people, and he had forbidden his wife to even mention her own encounter.

Suoma of Sedgebrook, Marjatta's mother, obeyed her husband in all things. She had married above her station, and it seemed to Marjatta that in her own home she was still a servant. She was a small, birdlike, fluttery woman, always busy, always nervous when Olaf was around.

"We're behind in the spinning and weaving," Suoma said. "And the loom shed will soon be too cold to work in. You know how your father hates it when we do the weaving in here." She looked around the room, which Marjatta now saw bore signs of disorder—pallets leaking straw and mending piled on chests—and spread her hands in a gesture of helplessness. "The walls need washing—I should have done it weeks ago—and the last batch of beer spoiled. It wasn't my fault, but you know how he—"

"Yes, I know." Marjatta removed her cloak and rolled up her sleeves. "What shall we start on first? And where are your maidservants?" When she had left for the mountains, there had been two.

Suoma sighed. "Your father keeps them both busy in the dairy. With all those new cows, the dairymaid can't manage alone."

It was a familiar lament. Olaf, who never hired enough workers, was always raiding the house servants, and Suoma would try to do all the work herself rather than complain to him.

They started on the walls, but had to stop to lay the table for supper. Olaf and the three men servants ate first, then Marjatta, her mother, and the three maids. After their meal the men returned to the farmyard to work until dark, and Suoma directed the maids to evening tasks in the house. On other farms, so Marjatta had heard, the entire household gathered at night in the big room for sociable talk and music and sometimes even dancing.

On Sedgebrook there was none of that. When Olaf came in he went straight to bed, and the women followed suit. Suoma joined her husband in the larger of the corner beds, and Marjatta took the other. The maids, whom she had displaced, settled themselves on pallets along the walls.

Later, when it was too cold in the outbuildings, the men servants would sleep in the house, too, on the benches. Marjatta thought wistfully of her solitude in the mountains. The closed-up room smelled stuffy, her father snored and one of the maids whimpered in her sleep.

The whimpering became a muffled sob. Marjatta located the source— it was Piltti, the newest and smallest maid: a thin, anxious-eyed child barely ten years old. Marjatta had thought her too young to be bound out, but according to Suoma she was better off with them than starving with her dirt-poor family.

When the sobbing continued, Marjatta rose and went to the child. "What is it, Piltti?" she whispered.

Piltti turned to the wall. "I wish I could go home," she mumbled.

"Here. Come." Marjatta raised her gently and led her to her own bed. "I miss my sisters, too," she whispered. "You can sleep here with me, if you like."

Piltti curled herself up under the furs, and after a moment she unburdened herself in a soft wail. "I spilled a pail of milk, and the master says if I do it again he'll switch me. It was Pekko's fault, he tripped me. He's always doing it, and I don't know how to make him stop!"

Marjatta patted the heaving shoulders. Pekko, she thought: the stable boy with the sly grin. "I'll speak to him," she promised. "It'll be all right. I'll see that he leaves you alone."

Piltti reached out her hand, and Marjatta squeezed it. "Who's doing all that talking?" Olaf growled sleepily from across the room. Piltti smothered a gasp and covered her head. Marjatta continued to pat her, and in a short time she was peacefully asleep.

Marjatta stayed awake longer, wondering how long she could continue to fit so easily into her old life. It was almost disappointing that no one had noticed a change in her—she who had been touched by a god! She rubbed her stomach and imagined the curled-up child within it, and in her mind he wore a tiny crown.

No one will ever hurt you, she vowed silently. He would never have a master like Olaf, be harrassed by stable boys, know hunger or fight in useless wars. Somehow, she would protect him from all that. She felt a flash of resentment with Tapio that he had left the entire burden to her. But . . . he must have deemed her capable. . . . With that comfort she fell asleep.

The next day she scolded Pekko and warned him against tormenting Piltti, and after that Marjatta acquired a devoted follower. The little maid leaped to do her every bidding and tried so assiduously to please her that even Olaf was impressed. "Maybe she'll make a decent servant after all," he allowed when Marjatta showed him the butter the child had produced from one day's churning. "Keep her at it."

The storehouses were well filled, but Olaf, never satisfied, was leaving soon for another raid on Pohjola. The men from Kaleva, led by the old sage Väinämöinen, the warrior Lemminkäinen and the smith Ilmarinen, had formed an army to storm Louhi's stronghold and bring back the Sampo. "Then you'll see all the granaries filled," Olaf promised as he polished his sword. "Why should they have all the good years?"

Maybe because they don't lose so many men in wars, Marjatta thought, but she didn't say it. Olaf was taking two of the men servants with him, leaving only Pekko to guard the women. "You have Marjatta," he said when Suoma made a feeble protest. "She can throw a spear as well as any man. Look at her—growing to look more like an ox every day. I've no fear leaving her in charge."

Marjatta's eyes stung at the words, but she was grateful he had no suspicions of the truth. An ox, was she? Her waist was indeed growing thicker, even though every morning she wound a long belt tightly under her dress. Suoma often looked at her strangely, but as yet she had said nothing.

Sometimes Marjatta liked the feeling that no one knew; it was a delicious, private joy that she hugged to herself. At other times she resented the secrecy. She should be cosseted, as other women were at such times, treated as someone special. She should be taken into the close sisterhood that she had always envied, not forced to hide and pretend.

The pretending became more difficult as the winter progressed. When Olaf left, snow was deep on the ground and the women were housebound, braving the outside cold only to tend to the cattle shut up in the barn. Marjatta spent as much time as she could there, bundled in furs, and she wore loose dresses in the house. The time came, however, when nothing could conceal the bulge of her belly.

"Shouldn't we be sewing swaddling bands?" Piltti whispered to her in bed one night. Marjatta hushed her, but she knew then that she would have to speak to Suoma.

"Of course I guessed," Suoma said the next morning. "Did you think I was blind? I hoped I was wrong, but . . . I'm just glad that your father. . . . "

She frowned and wrung her hands in her distress. "Whatever will he do, when he finds out? After all my warnings, how could you let this happen? You've no husband, and I'm afraid to even ask who the father is." Her face reddened as she paced a small circle. "Think of the shame, when people find out. Your father—he'll say it's all my fault, that I didn't bring you up right, that it's because of my low birth. He'll throw it up to me about my sister, the one who ran off with that horse thief. He'll—he'll"—she buried her face in her apron and uttered a long wail—"how could you, how *could* you!"

Suoma collapsed on the table bench, weeping. Marjatta sat beside her, staring at the wall, at a loss what to say or do. She felt a hand plucking her sleeve and turned to find Piltti regarding her with bright-eyed curiosity. "Who *is* the father?" the child asked.

Suoma stopped her crying and looked up, too. The other two maids came in with the milk, and Marjatta faced a battery of eyes.

She told her story calmly, without shame. Why was it a disgrace, to be chosen by a god? "He came to me in a dream," she said. "After I had eaten the berries. Then he came again, at the pool, and told me that the child would be a great king." She lifted her chin. "Believe me or not, I swear it's the truth. I'm sorry, Mother, for the trouble it may cause you. I won't be a burden. I'm strong, and even with the baby I'll do my share of work. About Father—we'll just have to wait and see. Maybe the baby will be here before he gets back, and he'll accept it. It's to be a boy, and he's always wanted an heir."

"Not that kind," Suoma said. "Not a base-born one. Forest god or not, you still have no husband."

"You believe me, then, about Tapio?"

Suoma rubbed her chin and frowned. "In the mountains—you swear you were alone all the time?"

Marjatta had a brief thought of Mikko the shepherd, but dismissed it as of no account. "Of course I was," she said.

"Then"—Suoma patted Marjatta's bulging stomach—"I'd say it's time we started sewing baby clothes."

Piltti clapped her hands and gave a small leap. The older maids exchanged looks of wry amusement. They didn't believe her, Marjatta suspected, but it really didn't matter. As long as her mother did. . . . She hugged Suoma, and the now-smiling woman turned red again.

Suoma's smiles became less frequent as the weeks passed and there was no word from Olaf. Marjatta's body grew heavier, until she could barely heave herself out of bed in the mornings. Every day she prayed that her pains would start, that the baby would be born before Olaf returned. Even with her mother's support, she didn't want to face him the way she was now. But with a beautiful, perfect baby in the cradle. . . .

106

Her prayers went unanswered. Olaf appeared at the farm gate on a day when the snow had turned to slush. He was on foot and alone, dirty and tattered and weaponless.

Marjatta hid in her bed, feigning illness, while Suoma welcomed her husband. "Get the sauna ready," is all he said in greeting, his mood was so foul. He scarcely glanced in Marjatta's direction.

His story came out in bits and curses and grunts: he had lost three good horses and two men, and come home empty-handed. The Kalevalanders had captured the Sampo, but had lost it on the way home, in a mighty sea-battle. "It rests now on the bottom of the ocean." He sounded immeasurably weary. "Maybe the fish will get some good out of it; for sure no men ever will."

"Did you see it—the Sampo?" Suoma asked, her eyes round.

Olaf nodded. "It didn't look like much to me. An ordinary grind-stone in a round kettle, with some kind of a fancy lid. Whatever magic it once had was long gone. Now, about that sauna. . . . "

Piltti came to tell him that the sauna was ready. Suoma went with him to be his water-thrower, and Marjatta rose and prepared a good meal. She hoped the food and the steam bath would put her father in a better mood, for she could delay her revelation no longer.

Olaf returned from the sauna red-faced but still scowling. "So, I see you're fatter than ever," he said to Marjatta. "We'll have to start rationing the butter before you eat us out of house and home."

Marjatta swallowed bitter words and turned sideways. Let him see it all, she thought. Let him get it over with.

Olaf's face froze, and he took a step backwards. "Hiisi take me, what is this?" He turned to his wife. "How long . . . what has been going on here? What kind of a joke is this?"

"It's no joke," Suoma said. "Marjatta is expecting a baby, very soon."

Olaf sat down abruptly. "Whose baby?"

Suoma looked at Marjatta. "Tell him."

Marjatta's mouth was as dry as tinder-moss as she told her story for the second time. With Olaf's flinty eyes boring into her, she knew how pre-posterous it sounded, and she stumbled over her words. "I know . . . it sounds crazy," she ended weakly.

"Yes, it does," he agreed. "I'm surprised you couldn't come up with a better invention. How about the truth?"

"It is the truth." Marjatta clenched her fists behind her back. *Please. Make him accept it.*

He snorted. "Do you take me for a fool?"

"Mother believes me," Marjatta said.

"Your mother would believe anything." Olaf's voice grew thick with sarcasm. "She even saw the Moonmaid."

"But . . . what Marjatta says has to be true," Suoma said timidly. She kept her eyes downcast. "She hasn't had anything to do with any man."

"Or so we thought." Olaf fixed Marjatta again with his piercing gaze. "What about those months on the mountain?"

"She was alone," Suoma said.

Olaf held up a hand. "Let *her* answer."

"I . . . I was alone," Marjatta affirmed.

"That may be," Olaf granted. "But before—there was Aulikki's wedding feast. All those guests, all that drinking." He rose and seized Marjatta by the shoulder. "You managed to slip away, didn't you? Off to the hay mow or the weaving shed." He shook her. "Didn't you?"

"No," she croaked. Her knees had turned to water, but she willed herself not to collapse.

"I say you did—I can see it in your face." He shook her again and shouted. "Now tell me who it was!"

Suoma plucked at Olaf's arm. "Please, please," she begged.

He shook her off. "Shameless whore!" he ranted on. "Hussy! The only way you could get a man, was it? Which drunken lowlife did you bed? I ought to kill him, but if he's unmarried I'll see that he takes you for a wife—a fit punishment. So speak!" He raised his hand as if to strike.

"It . . . it was Tapio," Marjatta said with chattering teeth. "I told you, it was Tapio, the forest spirit."

"Enough!" Olaf thundered. "No spirit made that belly. Now give me the truth, or you'll find no more shelter under this roof."

Marjatta feared he meant it. She knew his rages, when no one could reach him. "But . . . where can I go?" She crossed protective arms over her stomach. "It's almost my time. What will I do?"

"Go to *him*. Whoever it is you're protecting. Whatever married man. That's it, isn't it? You were stupid enough, or desperate enough, to lie with someone else's husband. Let *him* find you a pig hovel to live in. Let *him* support your bastard. I wash my hands of you." He made the symbolic gesture. "Now *go*! And I mean *now!*" He folded his arms, turned and stared into the fire pit. "I'm counting twelve breaths," he warned.

Suoma threw her apron over her head and wailed. The maids, all but Piltti, cowered in the bed-corners.

"I'm going with you," Piltti said to Marjatta. She gathered up the baby clothes and her few belongings. Marjatta, in a daze, made a pack of her own things. She pulled on her boots and wrapped her fur cloak around her.

"It's time," Olaf said. He didn't turn, and his voice was still laced with anger. "I don't want to see your face ever again. You or your brat. Not here, not ever."

Marjatta stumbled to the door, supported by Piltti. Suoma wailed louder, her cries audible almost all the way to the farthest gate.

Marjatta rested against the fence. The road was a mire of mud and half-melted snow, and the chill in the air promised a freeze that would soon make it impassable on foot. They had to move fast—but where? Marjatta's only concern was the safety of her child. She had to stay well, for his sake. She had to find shelter, and a clean, warm place to give birth. A sauna was too much to hope for, unless. . . . "Do you know the way to Ruotus' place?" she asked Piltti. The one-eyed man had no love for Olaf. Perhaps, out of spite, he might take them in.

"Yes, I can find it," Piltti said. "But aren't you coming?"

"I don't know if I can walk so far," Marjatta replied. "I'll go with you as far as I'm able, then you must run ahead and beg a place for us."

They started off, their boots sinking noisily into the slush. They hadn't gone far when they heard a halloo-ing from behind.

It was Suoma, running, her coat flapping and her house shoes a muddy ruin. Catching up, she thrust a bundle at Marjatta. "Here," she panted, "some food, a blanket and a few coins. He doesn't know."

Marjatta hugged her. "Is it all right about Piltti? Has he said anything?"

Piltti lifted her chin. "It doesn't matter. I'm going anyway."

"Take her," Suoma said. "But hurry." She waved them off.

"I'll try to get word to you, about the baby," Marjatta called back. She shifted her pack to her other shoulder and concentrated on putting one foot in front of the other. Her back ached and her legs were heavy as fence posts, but she trudged doggedly on.

Piltti, a ways ahead, turned often to encourage her. "It can't be much farther," the little maid said after it seemed to Marjatta they had been marching for hours. The sky was darkening, and an icy wind blew into their faces.

Marjatta staggered and nearly fell. "I can't go on," she said through numb lips. She looked around desperately. The snow was too wet to make a proper snow cave, but perhaps, under the not too distant grove of trees. . . . "I'll stop there," she said, pointing it out to Piltti. She tried to move, and couldn't. "But you'll have to help me."

Piltti peered, frightened, into Marjatta's strained face. "Mistress, please, don't be ill here," she begged.

The baby inside her gave a leap. *I won't let you come to harm,* Marjatta promised. From somewhere she summoned strength, and leaning on Piltti, crossed the open field to the stand of firs.

An empty hut nestled among the trees. An abandoned sheep shed, probably, Marjatta guessed. Part of the roof was fallen in, but inside, one end was dry and protected from the wind.

Piltti made her a bed on the earth floor. On her side, her hands clasping her drawn-up knees, Marjatta shivered under her fur cloak. A bolt of pain shot through her body, but she said nothing to further alarm Piltti. "Go quickly," she begged. "Tell Ruotus I'm desperate, that I must use his sauna." She felt around her for Suoma's pouch and held out one of the coins. "And I'll need a woman . . . his wife, if she will. Tell him it's urgent, that he should start the sauna fire now."

"You'll need a sledge, to get there," Piltti said. "I'll ask for that, too."

"Just hurry." Marjatta bit her lip against another pain. After Piltti left, she settled herself to wait. It would be a long process, she knew. A first birth always was. She had helped at Kerttu's, her middle sister's, and it had gone on for a night and a day. She remembered the scene in the hot, crowded bath house: the women chattering as they bustled about with rags and boiling water, Kerttu thrashing and screaming on the bench, the steam and the sweat and the smell of blood.

Marjatta's pains came and went. They seemed less severe now, and in between she even fancied she had imagined them. After a while she dozed, and Tapio's face was looking down on her.

A new day, he said.

Marjatta opened her eyes, expecting to see the morning, but it was still twilight. The face was gone.

He was outside, in the fir forest, Marjatta thought. It comforted her, knowing he was so near. When the pains returned, harder than before, she almost convinced herself that she wasn't afraid. Tapio had probably meant that the baby would be born the next day and that she should be patient. She loosened her clothing and tried to find a comfortable position, but each new wave left her gasping and praying that Piltti would come soon.

She gingerly touched her tight, swollen belly and tried to speak lovingly to the child, but when the white-hot rending came again she could only beg the babe to stop torturing her. She was glad no one was there to see her tears, and she wiped them hurriedly when she heard the sound of a horse, then voices, outside.

Piltti came in, accompanied by an old woman bundled in furs. "You got a sledge!" Marjatta, in her relief, half rose from the floor. "Thank the gods for Ruotus!"

"Don't waste your breath," the old woman said in a cracked voice. "That one deserves no thanks. I couldn't believe the stingy old wolf, or his wife, that they could be so heartless."

"They were afraid of my master," Piltti said. "When I told them who you were, that he had cast you out, they refused to help."

"Heartless," the granny-woman repeated. "I said to him, I'll go to the poor thing, and he'd better let me have a horse." She cackled. "He thinks I know witch-ways, and that I could curse him, so he lets me stay in his house, old and and useless as I am." She pushed back her hood and bent over Marjatta. "Useless I may be to him, but I've birthed many a babe, and I can still do it, so don't you worry, my sweeting."

In the dim light, the woman's wrinkled, toothless face did not inspire confidence, but as another wave of rending pain hit her, Marjatta gratefully pulled on the bony hands.

"Let's see what's happening," the woman said when the pain had passed. She parted Marjatta's legs and peered between them, clucking and murmuring. "We'll need a fire," she said to Piltti, directing her where to dig the pit and place stones. The little maid used wood from the fallen portion of the roof, and before it was totally dark the hut was warmed and lighted.

The old woman—"Laina the lovely," she said with another hoarse chortle—unpacked her birthing bundle and soon had herbs steeping in boiling water, cloths laid out, and twine and a sharp knife. When she stirred her pots and threw water on the stones, steam and a spicy smell permeated the makeshift sauna.

Marjatta paced, supported by Piltti, until the pains forced her off her feet. Laina made a clean, soft place for her to lie down and told her to scream all she liked. "There's no one to hear," she said, "and it may frighten the babe into coming sooner."

Marjatta, however, thought of Tapio out in the woods and stifled her cries. She didn't want him to think her weak, so she gnawed her lips and clutched the edges of her blanket in her damp hands. After every fit of pain the sweat poured from her, but Laina insisted she stay covered. When she thrashed too much, the old woman made a rope of twisted cloth and fastened it to a knot on the wall.

Marjatta pulled, and when she could bear it no longer she forgot about Tapio and screamed. She threw up Laina's bitter potion, which was supposed to bring relief. The pains came faster, until between bouts she barely had time to recover before another wave engulfed her.

It went on and on, and Marjatta lost all sense of time. Surely it was taking too long, she thought. After what seemed an eternity she had no more strength to pull on the rope, and the pain was nearly constant. Dimly, through a red fog, she heard Piltti sobbing and Laina muttering angrily. The granny-woman pressed on her stomach, and Marjatta thought she would surely die from the agony.

"There's one thing I can try," Laina said as she wiped Marjatta's face. "It may seem strange, but I saw it done once and it loosened the babe."

"Anything," Marjatta whispered.

Laina went outside. After a moment she reappeared at the door of the hut, leading the horse. Marjatta knew a flash of panic—what did the woman intend?—but she was helpless in her pain and could only watch and wait.

"Help me hold him," Laina said to Piltti, and together they brought the struggling animal inside and positioned it in front of Marjatta. "Breathe on her," the old woman commanded. She uncovered Marjatta's belly. "Let your breath blow over her," she chanted. "Breathe the vapor of life on this mother and child."

The horse whinnied and puffed out a cloud of steam. When the vapor settled on Marjatta's stomach, she felt something shift within her and for a miraculous moment she was eased. Then, before she could speak, the pain grabbed her and she pushed so violently that it seemed she must be turning inside out.

Laina directed Piltti to pull Marjatta to a squatting position. The horse stamped and whinnied, and to Marjatta's disordered mind she was trapped in a nightmare of screaming witches and wildly cavorting beasts. She was being tortured, rent in two, and she could do nothing to stop it.

"Push," the witch said, grinning evilly into Marjatta's face. A final, huge, impossible pain took her, and she knew she would not survive it.

She collapsed into Piltti's arms.

She was dead, she thought. Feather-light, and waiting to cross Tuoni's river. When Laina brought her a red, squalling bundle she thought it must be some further horror.

"A healthy boy," Laina said.

Marjatta returned to the world. "Let me see." She held out her arms.

The horse continued to whinny and stamp until Piltti succeeded in getting it outside. The baby stopped crying, and it was suddenly quiet in the hut. A bright, full moon shone through the doorway, and Marjatta saw her newborn son bathed in an unearthly glow. *It had all come true.* She loosened the swaddling and gazed with awe at the tiny, perfect form. "Isn't he wonderful?" she breathed.

Laina chuckled. "He looks like an ordinary baby. A bit scrawny, perhaps, but they always improve."

Marjatta gasped. *Ordinary! Scrawny!* Was the woman blind? Couldn't she see that the child was beyond beautiful?

Piltti came to look, and marvelled enough to satisfy Marjatta. Laina built up the fire, scolded Marjatta for unwrapping the baby, and soon had both mother and child bundled snugly. "That'll do, for now," she worried aloud, "but what's to become of the pair of you? Castoffs, without even a decent roof over your heads. What are you to do when it rains? And where will your food come from?"

Marjatta closed her eyes and sank into a blissful half sleep. Dimly she heard Laina's mutterings, but their substance did not affect her. *Greater than any of us,* Tapio had said. She repeated it to herself. Surely, Laina had no cause to worry.

*   *   *

> He was growing up so handsome,
> Beautiful son of Marjatta.
> No one knew what name to give him,
> Knew the proper name to call him.
>
> *The Kalevala,* Runo 50

Fortunately it didn't rain before Pekko came from Sedgebrook to repair the roof of the shed. Suoma sent food, too, secretly, and even slipped away herself to admire the baby.

Olaf refused to come. "I'm sure he knows where I am," Suoma said on one of her visits, "but we both pretend he doesn't." Every time she came, Suoma brought some new improvement for the hut—today, a cloth for the rough table Marjatta and Piltti had hammered together. There was fresh straw covering the dirt floor, a box cradle for the baby, and a working firepit with a smoke-hole in the new roof.

Suoma rocked the baby in her arms. She and Marjatta sat beside the fire while Piltti hung up washing in the other end of the shed. "Your father hardly speaks to me," Suoma continued. "He's still angry about you, but more, I think, about the way the war turned out. The men all are. We've had more of them than I can count, sick and wounded, stopping off at the house. Väinämöinen is there now, and he has scarcely a word to say for himself."

"I find that hard to believe," Marjatta said, remembering how the old spellsinger loved to talk.

"It's true." The baby fussed, and Suoma lifted him to her shoulder. "Väinämöinen's . . . changed. I asked him if he'd do a naming ceremony for this little one, and he said the most awful things."

"Because the baby has no father—no *human* father?"

"Maybe, but I don't think it's just that. I think it's the business about losing the Sampo. He said it would be better for the boy if he hadn't been born, and that he ought to be drowned in a swamp." Suoma shuddered. "He must expect awful times ahead."

Marjatta's anger flared. "Drowned in a swamp! How dare he!" She took the baby from her mother and held him tightly. "As for bad times coming, they're his fault. What has Väinämöinen done for us? We've had nothing but wars and more wars, and for all his so-called magic we're no better off."

Suoma put a warning finger to her lips, though there was no one to overhear. "He can still curse you, or the babe. I begged him to come here and at least take a look at the little one. When he sees that sweet face . . . he'll have to give him a proper blessing."

"He *must*." Marjatta gazed fiercely, lovingly, at her small son. Väinämöinen, for all his defeats and failing powers, was the one person to assure that the child wouldn't remain an outcast. A simple blessing. . . . "I'd go to him myself, if it weren't for Father."

"No, don't come to the house. I can't answer for what Olaf might do." Suoma puckered her brow. "But there has to be a way."

Marjatta thought, too. "How is Väinämöinen traveling? By sleigh or by boat?"

"By boat." Suoma's face lit up. "I could let you know when he's leaving, and you could meet him at the beach. You and the babe. I'll send Pekko with a sled. Olaf won't need to know, and you can get that old granny-woman—Laina, is it?—for a witness. Does she still come around?"

"Yes, she's been a big help." Tapio had sent her, Marjatta firmly believed. Without her and Piltti, she and the baby might not have survived. The forest god was still watching over her—she sensed him every day—but she no longer spoke of him to Suoma.

"Are you sure about the father?" Suoma had asked the first time she saw the child. He had been red-faced from crying, with a soiled breech-cloth. She hadn't seen in him the features of a god, but only Marjatta's nose and an odd-shaped finger that she said came from her own family.

Suoma hadn't pressed her, and when Marjatta saw how her mother loved the baby she forgave her her doubts. She had thought once that everyone would immediately guess the child's divine parentage, and it was a disappointment that they didn't, but she told herself that Tapio must have his reasons for clouding their eyes.

They continued to discuss the name ceremony. "I'll come, too, if I can," Suoma said. "We'll try to have it done properly. Have you settled yet on what to call him?"

Marjatta shook her head. She had considered all the names she had ever heard, and none seemed right; none was noble enough for such an exceptional child. "Perhaps I'll let Väinämöinen choose one," she said. "From one of his songs." Her voice grew dreamy. "The name of a great hero."

Suoma smiled and rose to leave. "I'll send word, then. I don't think it'll be long—Väinämöinen will want to get home for his spring planting. Be ready to come quickly."

After her mother left, Marjatta put the baby to sleep in his cradle and went outside to gather firewood. It was a task she enjoyed, especially now that the forest was beginning to awaken from winter. It was dry under the trees, and in their dappled green shade she often felt Tapio very near. He never showed himself, however, and this day she didn't even sense his presence.

Something was disturbing the peace of the forest. Small animals scurried from tree to tree, and from overhead came a rush of wings. A bear, Marjatta thought, and frost crawled up the back of her neck, under her skin. At a crashing noise she dropped her armload of branches and ran, but before she could go far a horse and rider broke through the underbrush.

The man leaped from his horse. "I'm sorry—please—I didn't mean to frighten you."

The voice sounded familiar. It sounded like . . . but it couldn't be. The intruder moved into a patch of sunlight, and Marjatta saw that it was indeed Mikko the shepherd. His scraggly beard was a bit fuller, and he seemed to have grown taller, but the shy, somewhat crooked smile and the green eyes were the same. "Wha—what are you doing here?" she stammered.

"Looking for you," he said.

She closed her gaping mouth. "I don't understand. Why . . . when?" She remembered the way he had run when she had shown herself and disclosed who she was. "I thought you'd be halfway across the world by now."

"I almost was. But I kept thinking what a coward I was, and I came back. Then, in the village, I heard about you, and the baby. I was so ashamed. What must you think of me!" He stared at the ground, his reddening face a pattern of misery. "I wonder if you can ever forgive me."

"Forgive you for what?" His embarrassment spread to her, arousing old hurts that she would rather not think about. He wasn't the first man to run from her; why should he make so much of it?

"Everything. The way I left." He wouldn't meet her eyes. "I was afraid for my life when I knew who your father was. Especially after . . . you know."

"No, I don't know." She couldn't help being short with him, the way he seemed to imply there had been something between them. "After what? My father would only have thanked you for taking care of me."

He looked up, finally, his eyes deeply puzzled. "I meant, after what happened in the night."

"That you held my hand? I wouldn't have told Father."

"You really don't remember?" He appeared transfixed with amazement.

"Remember what?" There had been all those embarrassing Tapio dreams, but he knew nothing about them. Or would ever need to know. All the same, she was strangely—unaccountably—frightened. Whatever knowledge he thought he posessed, she wanted no more revelations. She wished he would leave.

Mikko twisted his cap in his hands, his color coming and going. He drew a breath. "What about the baby? I heard there was one."

She started to lie, then suddenly was ashamed of herself. What did she have to fear from him? "Come on; I'll show you," she said. She didn't know why he was acting so oddly, but she and the baby needed every friend. And he had been kind to her, after all, when she was ill. "How did you find me?" she asked as they walked through the forest.

"A woman in the village," he said. "She knew where you were living, how your father cast you out. When I heard that, I thought, 'I can offer her something better than a sheep shed.' I know I'm not anyone your father would approve of, but I can always find work, even with my bad leg. It would have to be somewhere away from here, maybe in Väinölä." His eyes met hers, briefly. "What would you think of that? I'd never have dared think of it myself, before, but now. . . . " His voice drifted off, as if he had lost courage.

She stopped in her tracks and stared at him. "What is it you're offering me?"

He swallowed. "I . . . I thought you might need a husband. I thought, maybe, you . . . I thought we might marry."

His words hung in the air. She wondered if she had misunderstood. Or if he had. "You know that my father has disowned me," she said. "That there would be no profit in it for you."

"I know."

"Well." She could think of nothing else to say. What could she say? It was so unexpected. So unsettling. There was so much to consider. She could only repeat, stupidly, "Well."

He cleared his throat. "You'll think about it?"

"I guess I can do that," she granted. They continued walking, he leading the horse. When they came to the shed, he tied the horse within the shelter of the trees. "I don't want anyone to know I'm here," he said. "Not Ruotus, the way I ran out on him, and especially not your father."

Marjatta nodded. She didn't want his presence known, either. Piltti regarded him curiously when they went inside, but Marjatta offered no explanation. "There he is," she said, pointing to the sleeping infant.

Mikko knelt and looked long at the child. Marjatta couldn't tell from his face what he was thinking. She told herself that it shouldn't matter to her, but still, she held her breath.

When they were outside again, the shepherd frowningly regarded the tips of his shoes before he addressed Marjatta. "So whose do you say he is?"

Marjatta stiffened. She was weary of telling the tale; weary of polite smiles of disbelief or ruder, scoffing responses. "Can't you *see*?" She didn't attempt to disguise her exasperation.

"No," he admitted. "I thought I'd recognize . . . some feature. But then, he's so little."

"You'd hardly recognize him for what he is," she said coldly. "No one seems to. I suppose they're not used to seeing a spirit child, a son of the forest god."

His mouth gaped. "Say that again?"

"I don't need to—you heard me!" Hot tears scalded her eyes. "I guess you think I'm crazy, like most people do. I guess you'll want to . . . forget about what you said before."

He clasped her shaking hands. "No, I don't want to forget it and I don't think you're crazy. But you *were* ill, up there on the mountain. You were sicker, I think, than I suspected."

She jerked her hands away. "I know what you're trying to say. And I *didn't* imagine it. I ate the berry, and I *saw* Tapio, and I talked to him. And there's the baby, there's the proof."

"Yes, proof," he agreed. He looked at her sadly.

"I suppose you'll be going, now." She continued to hold herself stiffly. Why should it matter to her, what he thought? She wished he hadn't come. She wished he would go quickly, like he had done before.

"No, I'm not leaving," he said. "I'll make a camp there in the woods, if it's all right with you."

She shrugged. "It's not my land."

"We'll talk later, then." He moved off, into the trees, and Marjatta returned to the hut. Piltti was full of questions, but Marjatta gave only short replies. Her breasts ached, and she wished the baby would waken. Studying him, she wondered why no one else could see the signs of greatness. Her nose and brow, that she had always so hated, on him she could already see as noble and commanding. His hands, even with the one crooked finger, were obviously made for grasping a scepter.

If only Mikko had seen it, she would have had no hesitancy in accepting his proposal. But he was like all the rest, and she couldn't imagine what he was thinking, out there in the woods.

The baby woke, and she sat in the doorway to nurse him. She looked for a curl of smoke in the woods, and spotted one not far away. So, this time the shepherd hadn't run off. She wondered if he had food, if she should send him some of hers. She was about to call to Piltti to make up a bundle when a horse and sled turned off the road and came bumping across the field.

It was Pekko. "Väinämöinen's leaving," he announced importantly. "He's on his way to the beach now, and mistress says for you to hurry."

Marjatta cut short the baby's meal and flew to dress him in his white robe. She wrapped a cloak about her own unchanged clothes and took her place in the sled behind Pekko. Piltti begged to come too, but Pekko said her weight would only slow them up, and Marjatta had to agree. They had miles to go, and Väinämöinen had a head start.

"Is he alone?" Marjatta asked as they sped along. If Väinämöinen had no help, he would be a while launching his boat.

"Not that one," Pekko answered with a grin. "He's got half the countryside to see him off."

She might have expected it. At least, Marjatta thought, there would be plenty of witnesses for the naming.

If there were a naming. "Take the shortcut," she urged, pointing where to leave the road. They jounced and nearly tipped, then plowed through a wet field. Mud flew from the sled runners as they crossed more fields and skirted forests, and as they approached the coast the ground grew even soggier. The baby suckled under the cloak and then slept, and Marjatta rehearsed what she would say to Väinämöinen.

The horse labored over a series of sedgy hills, and topping the last one, they came to the sea.

A dozen or so people were gathered on the rocky shore. Väinämöinen, his beard blowing in the breeze, directed the four men who were pushing the boat, but there seemed to be so much dissention among them that they were making little progress. The others on the beach were arguing as well, their angry voices raised in a cacophony of insults. Marjatta's heart sank when she recognized the most vociferous of the quarrelers, a man easily half a head taller than the others. It was her father.

She couldn't have had worse luck, she thought as she climbed out of the sled. She stood a ways back, waiting to be recognized, but the shouting men scarcely glanced at the new arrivals.

Olaf was squared against his neighbor Ruotus, both men waving fists. "Don't call me a coward!" Olaf roared. "I was there, I lost two men in the fighting. I wasn't sitting safe at home like you. You're the one who's a coward, and you've no right to even open your mouth about the war!"

"I've every right!" the short, burly man roared back. He pointed to his eyepatch. "I lost that fighting the damned witch, and everyone knows it. Everyone knows, too, that I'd have gone again this time if I hadn't been laid low with a fever."

"You and how many others?" someone else shouted. "Ask Väinämöinen—we'd have won if we'd had more men!"

Väinämöinen raised both hands in the air. "Enough! I've had enough of fighting, enough for a lifetime, and I won't listen to more of it here!"

The tumult died to angry mutters, but Olaf and Ruotus continued to glare at one another. "More or less men, it wouldn't have made any difference," Väinämöinen said. "The war was ill-fated."

"So what are we going to do now?" Ruotus growled. "Slink off like a pack of whipped curs?"

"I suggest we let it rest." Väinämöinen seemed to have aged a decade since Marjatta had last seen him, his shoulders now slumped with fatigue and his face etched with new, deep lines of disillusionment. "Louhi suffered losses, too. I don't think she'll be bothering us for a while."

Olaf gripped Väinämöinen's arm. "I still think *some* people ought to be fined. For sitting fat and safe while others risked their lives. What do you say?"

"That it has nothing to do with me." Väinämöinen shook off the restraining hand and proceeded to his boat, which was still half on the sand. On the way, he noticed Marjatta and turned back to Olaf. "So here's your daughter. Maybe you should be mending your own fences instead of making new quarrels." He shook his head. "I said, I've had enough of contentions."

Marjatta came forward and showed the old spellsinger the baby. "I was hoping you'd give him a name and a blessing. He's special, you know. A gift from a god."

"A god!" Olaf snorted, then cursed and started toward Marjatta. "Didn't I tell you to stay away? Haven't you shamed me enough?"

Väinämöinen waved him back. "She has a rightful request." He studied the baby's face. "A gift from a god?" he said after a long moment. "Maybe he is. What do I know of the ways of gods? What do any of us know?"

Marjatta scarcely dared breathe. "Then you'll give him a suitable name?" she finally ventured. "I leave the choice to you."

"In that case, I'll try to do him justice." He took the baby from her and gazed at him again. His mouth twitched, but his eyes were profoundly serious. "I name you, 'Kalevan Kuningas,'" he said as he traced the outline of a crown on the tiny curving forehead.

Kalevan Kuningas. Marjatta mouthed the words, her eyes wide. It was more than she had expected. *King of Kaleva.*

Gasps came from the onlookers. "Is that a name or a title?" someone asked.

"Both," Väinämöinen replied. "May he be the one to bring peace to our country."

"Do you have a song for him?" Marjatta asked as she received her new-named son back into her arms.

Someone handed Väinämöinen his harp. "Yes, a song," came murmurs from the crowd.

Väinämöinen shook his head and passed the harp to Marjatta. "Keep it for him. I have no more songs." His face settled into a mask of pain and resignation. "Let a new poet sing songs of mightier magic. For the coming generation. For a new day."

The old singer pushed the boat easily into the water and leaped in. Without a backward look he steered into the open sea.

"Now what did that mean?" came the murmurs.

"A king? He must have seen something I missed." It was Laina, who had shouldered her way from the back of the crowd. She peered curiously at the child. "Well . . . perhaps," she granted. She placed a small embroidered cap on the sand beside the harp. "It so happens I have something for the little one."

Others began to search their pockets and the contents of their sleds, until the gifts formed a small pile. Marjatta looked for Olaf, but he was gone. No matter, she hadn't expected acceptance from him. She turned to watch Väinämöinen until he was nothing but a dot on the calm gray sea.

Suddenly, he was gone. He would have kept to the shore if he were going home, Marjatta thought. They wouldn't see him again. She clutched her son and turned back to the land, to the thawing fields and the budding trees and the now quiet people. To Mikko waiting in the forest.

*   *   *

"Let the rope of time run out—
One day go, another come."

The Kalevala, Runo 50